SHADOW

SEALs of Honor, Book 5

Dale Mayer

Books in This Series:

SHADOW: SEALS OF HONOR, BOOK 5
Dale Mayer
Valley Publishing

Copyright © 2016

ISBN-13: 978-1-928122-83-8
Print Edition

Back Cover

Shadow's life has been an uphill struggle. No wonder he's so damn good at dealing with the hard, the difficult, and the dangerous.

Shadow's all about being a SEAL. The one world he's comfortable in. He knows what he can do, when to do it, and how to do it ... until he sets off on a mission to rescue Arianna and her family, and his world goes from controlled action to chaos. Who knew women like her existed?

Arianna struggles to deal with the foreign world she's been plunged into. Kidnappings, beatings, threats. *SEALs.* The only good thing is the darkest, most dangerous-looking saviour she's ever met. And he doesn't know what to do with her.

Well, she has a good idea, but will they get that chance? Not if the kidnappers have anything to say about it.

Arianna has been marked for extinction, and it's up to Shadow to save her ... before it's too late and he loses something he had no idea he wanted in the first place ... but now he can't live without.

Sign up to be notified of all Dale's releases here!

http://dalemayer.com/category/blog/

COMPLIMENTARY DOWNLOAD

DOWNLOAD a ***complimentary*** copy of TUESDAY'S CHILD? Just tell me where to send it! http://dalemayer.com/starterlibrarytc/

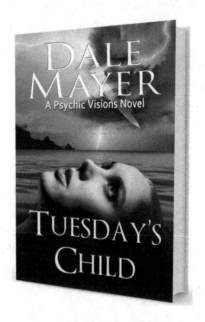

CHAPTER 1

JAMES MORROW, SHADOW to his friends, watched the lake come into view below him. He leaned forward to peer through the cockpit of the small bush plane he'd been riding in for the last half hour. This wasn't how he'd expected to be traveling. None of his team had. Mechanical trouble had brought their military helicopter to an emergency landing. Shitty timing. They were on a mission. To rescue a US senator and his family being held hostage in a remote Canadian cabin.

Instead they'd been the ones in need of assistance. They managed to land close to a small town, but without enough time to bring in a second military aircraft, and time being of an essence, they'd ended up in one of those small bush planes barely able to handle the weight of the four passengers fully geared. Dane and Swede were traveling with the Canadian unit in a different aircraft along with Markus and Evan, two other SEALs that were part of this mission. Good men. Shadow had worked with both before. Actually at this point, he'd been lucky enough to work with several dozen SEALs. It was just over time some were more memorable than others. Markus had lost his wife in his first year at Coronado. A loss that had hurt him deeply. It had been easy to empathize. That he'd kept his head down and his focus on his work, well, he'd earned everyone's respect then.

Evan was a bit of a wild card. Divorced and possibly had a death wish with all his explosives training. Shadow was good, but Cooper and Evan rocked that world.

That didn't mean he was giving up his position though. Shadow was in the passenger seat for once – where he could see for miles. The others were in the cargo hold. Interesting switch. Then as a SEAL, he was accustomed to change. And being prepared. And adapting. One had to.

Hopefully the senator's family was holding up to the devastation in their life as well. There'd been no demands as yet. But the adult daughter had managed to transmit a blurry photo of one man to the senator's aide in Washington after they'd arrived at the cabin, and that had been enough for both countries to jump into action. The man was a known terrorist. In fact, he sat at the top of the top Ten Most Wanted list.

Not that Shadow cared about the list.

Shadow cared about the job. The work he did. This was his life. He was a remote cabin in the woods kind of guy. Take the city out of his world and he was at peace. Living on the base was a necessity, but he got away every chance he could. His friend and SEAL brother, Hawk, jointly owned a ranch with his sister several hours out of Coronado. Something Shadow could see himself doing. Only he knew Hawk and his sister were involved in heavy discussions about their options as they both had long term relationships to make work and the living arrangements needed some rethinking. Hawk had partnered up with his sister's best friend. And Shadow's best friend Swede had partnered up with Hawk's sister. Confusing, maybe, but it worked for them.

Then Shadow had seen that relationship coming. Hard not to. Only poor Swede, that big mountain hadn't.

Talk about being blind.

The way Swede had looked at Eva all these years but knowing it was a place he couldn't go…yeah painful. Still, they'd finally gotten there. Even if it had taken a rebel training camp and a mess of rescued horses to bring them together. Shadow grinned. It would take something like that for the big guy to make his move. But he was so damn happy now, it was ridiculous. That soured his mood instantly. Almost all his friends were happily paired up. It was almost sickening.

The small plane was buffeted by the heavy winds. Lightning cracked outside the window. He frowned, studying the thunderclouds around him. They should be close. The bush plane was rigged with floats, the plan to scoop down on the nearest lake and drop them as close to shore as Bob, the pilot, could get them to where the senator's family was being held. The storm gave them wonderful coverage for the landing. The plane engine would be lost in the crackle of the lightning and thunder. No one should be out in this nasty weather.

They were also landing further away from the cabin than the family would have arrived. They couldn't take the chance of alerting the kidnappers of their arrival.

Shadow looked at his SEAL team behind him, seeing that air of intense focus. That air of expectancy. That understanding of why they were here. That something could go wrong. Likely would go wrong. And they'd be ready. Whether it was Mother Nature about to unleash her worst on their small tin box in the sky or the terrorists holding the senator's family down below in the darkness – they had a job to do and they loved it.

So did he.

Being a SEAL had given him purpose. He'd needed that. He

hated to admit it but joining the navy, coming from a small town to the city of the military had been tough. But he'd bore down and survived – thrived actually.

Yet there'd been always a sense of separation inside. As if the only way he could manage to get through this was to keep himself detached. Lock off the inner part of himself that was held inviolate. Foolish he knew. Particularly as he'd watched his friends go through such upheavals in their lives. They each let someone special inside. He didn't think he could. His walls were too strong. Too high. Too old.

The plane rocked wildly in the wind.

The pilot slowly descended, trying to bring the plane below the heavy cloud cover as visibility was nonexistent. And the plane wasn't equipped with the latest or the best equipment. Shadow half suspected that the old geezer beside him could fly this thing blindfolded. He had a special gift. A rare connection to his "girl."

Shadow understood.

He'd seen many an old-timer connect to a boat or car, or in this case a plane, in such a way that they seemed to have a surreal relationship. As Shadow watched, Bob coaxed the small plane down at a gentle descent. Shadow couldn't see all the dials on the dashboard but the one he could see, the altimeter, was spinning like mad. So the instruments had been affected by the storm too. He wasn't nervous. He was in life and death situations often. But not normally due to Mother Nature.

The clouds thinned enough to show the deep blue of a lake below, dancing in and out of their view as they descended. Good. This was the right lake. They'd be landing soon. He hoped the water was calmer than it looked.

It wasn't. As they got almost to the water level he could see white caps whipping up below them.

"Gonna be close," the pilot said with a huge tobacco stained toothy grin. "But you guys live for close, don't you?" His grin widened, but his gaze never came off the water as he carefully brought the old girl in to as smooth a float landing as possible given the circumstances.

Shadow respected the casual skill with which Bob set the plane down on the angry waves. This man had seen a lot of years in this type of wilderness in all kinds of weather to do what he'd just done. With no pier or dock to tie up to, the plane bobbed to the far end and Bob shut down the engines. The small plane rocked gently. Shadow looked at the shoreline and realized they were only about thirty feet out. Nice.

He turned to the back of the plane in time to see a small inflatable raft being lowered to the water and the first of his team climbing down into it. The raft was large enough to hold all four of them, but only just.

At the shore, they disembarked and turned to watch as Bob's winch rewound the rope still attached to the inflatable then he struggled to reload the boat in the cargo hold. Once done, he was quick to get back to the cockpit and turn on the engines.

The plane took off and disappeared into the storm clouds.

Good. They were alone.

Just the way they liked it.

Now to save the senator.

CHAPTER 2

ARIANNA STEPHENSON HUDDLED by the fire in the corner of the large cabin. Her baby brother had crawled half into her lap, his head nestled against her shoulder. At eight, he had just enough understanding of the world around them to know they were in big trouble. She'd always been fun and lighthearted with him, but there was no making light of this.

Her father, his head brightly colored after being battered by the kidnappers at the outset, sat on the couch, silent, his face pinched. But she didn't know if that was from the pain or the situation. Her beautiful stepmother sat beside her father, fingers and lips trembling and tears constantly pouring into the Kleenex crumpled in her hand.

Arianna might have more sympathy if her stepmother didn't look this way after most upsets, particularly when Arianna or Kevin refused to do her bidding. At his young age, Kevin had already taken more after his big sister's temperament than his mother wanted.

Yet if there was ever going to be a situation where her step-mother's reaction was appropriate – it was this one. And how stupid really. She'd been pulling that play for a decade now, and Arianna had come to the point of smiling sweetly and bringing her another box of Kleenex. Only this time it was for real, and

Arianna didn't know how to deal with her.

Her father had been a senator for eighteen years. They'd had some security issues in the middle of that reign, but things had settled down in these last few years, at least she thought so. She hadn't lived at home for many years now so didn't live under the constant pressure she had when living there.

When they'd boarded a small plane to come to her grandfather's cabin in the Canadian wilderness, they'd had a very unpleasant reception waiting for them upon landing. They'd been marched from the dock to the cabin at gunpoint. As it was summer, and she wasn't due back at her teaching job until September, Arianna and Kevin had big plans to enjoy the unusual holiday. If she hadn't come, Kevin would be alone. Eight and having to listen to his mother bug their father every minute of the day. She was nothing if not contrary. Their father had done his best with Kevin when he'd been younger, but they'd grown apart years ago and now her father was always busy. She understood. The relationship followed the same pattern she'd gone through. She didn't want that for Kevin. She had lots of great memories of the land around the cabin she wanted to show him.

But who knew they'd be taken hostage? She stared out at the trees blowing wildly across the windows. A hell of a storm raged outside. Even considering they were under armed guard she was glad to be inside. She loved the outdoors as much as anyone but in a storm like this, it would turn nasty very quickly.

Except a storm raged inside, too.

She hoped her message had gotten through. Her phone had been ripped from her hands as soon as she'd hit send and crushed on the floor in front of her. All phones had been confiscated. So they had no way to call for the plane to pick them up early. It was prearranged for the same pilot to return on Monday.

But that was a lifetime away.

Her cheek still stung from the blow she'd received for sending the image. But it was nothing compared to what it could be. The leader had seemed to think her attempts more hilarious than anything. The terrorists wanted something from her father. His vote on something to do with oil. She remembered vaguely that there was an even split on the decisions that had been announced so far. Her father had yet to announce his decision. She wasn't even sure which side of the issue he was coming down on. Given his past views though, it was likely on the no side. He had no interest in oil pipelines anywhere across the country. Figured they weren't worth the environmental damage should something happen. But it was an unpopular decision for many as it would create thousands of jobs and of course that was a hot issue.

That's why she avoided politics like the plague. Her father had been approached with bribes, no...gifts, they called it, ever since his appointment had been announced. If he had been offered bribes for a vote in one direction or another then it made sense that someone would think he could be coerced one way or another as well. The old "if I can't give you a kiss then I'll give you a kick" sentiment. If she wasn't being watched so closely, she'd have laughed at her twist on the old attention getting action.

Still, she hadn't planned to spend her holiday facing guns. And what the hell kind were they anyway? Something like an assault rifle. They were mean looking firearms. And that was a whole different story. These guys were pros.

And she was stuck here waiting for a rescue.

Only she didn't do the whole damsel in distress thing very
well. In fact, she wasn't sure she rocked the damsel thing at all.
She was tall and lean and more athletically built than her women
friends. As in missing the coveted junk in front and in the back.
She was greyhound sleek, but her B cups didn't look as bountiful
as her friends' chests. They'd been trying to convince her to get a
boob job, but she'd laughed and said hell no. The men needed to
take her the way she was or forget it. She didn't need a guy to
want her for the silicone in her chest. And the concept of a butt
implant grossed her out. She was what she was. And damn it,
apparently that wasn't good enough.

Staring into the flames, stuck under guard, she realized how
stupid it was to worry about her past lovers or physical failings –
at least according to the men she'd dated – given her current
situation. But it helped keep her mind off her worries. Another
had wanted her to have curvy hips to shake on a dance floor, but
he was out of luck there too. Why couldn't she attract marathon
runners? After all that's what she was. She had no desire to return
after an exhilarating run to someone still sitting on the couch.

"Love you, honey, be back in couple of hours." Then go run
your heart out and feel the blood pumping through your veins
like there wasn't going to be any tomorrow and come home to
find the honey still sitting and playing video games? So not her
style. Then, she didn't do video games either.

Kevin shifted in her arms. She smiled. She hadn't played
them growing up. Her mother hadn't been a believer in any
entertainment that required electronics. She'd learned to play
video games for her kid brother. It was a great day when he could
kick her butt on a game. He led a lonely life. And Arianna had
done her best, but she couldn't be there all the time for him. Her

stepmother was overprotective. Always afraid Kevin would get hurt. Of course, he had a hearing problem and speech impediment, but he was neither deaf nor dumb. But it made him a target by other kids. It helped to develop a tough skin early on.

Then kids were cruel and nothing protected anyone all the time.

Arianna was of the opinion that small hurts weren't a bad thing in the long run. Kevin's small hand snuck into hers. She wrapped an arm around him and tugged him so he was sitting between her legs and leaning back against her. He nestled in close. She studied the guard on the left. Bored to hell and stuck on his cell phone like so many people today. Did he have cell reception? Would his phone work to send out a message or just to play the correct flavor of the month game that everyone glommed onto?

She nudged Kevin, a budding techie, toward the guard's activities. She could see he didn't understand what he was looking at until his gaze landed on the phone and the information processing behind his thick Coke bottle glasses made his eyes glisten. Now he was thinking.

She squeezed him reassuringly. With a casual glance around she studied her father's grim demeanor and her stepmother's distress. They didn't look like they were going to be of any help. She worried about her father's condition. He didn't look well. He wasn't a well man to begin with. He had his first heart attack seven years ago, another small one a couple of years ago. Another man stood at the back behind them all. He caught her looking at him and raised the gun barrel to point at her. She flipped back around. She had yet to see the terrorist she'd managed to photograph again.

Her heart pounded inside her chest and it took minutes for her panic to ease back. They'd been here close to ten hours now. How much longer until something happened? There was a four by four parked outside, but she knew the keys were in the pocket of the guy with the cell phone. Was there a second set to be found? She assessed the men. There'd been four at the cabin when they'd arrived. But there were more than that here now only she didn't know how many more. She'd thought it was only fly in and fly out access but old roads crisscrossed the area so it made sense that they'd have driven more men in if they could.

And that was encouraging. Road access also meant an escape route.

Kevin whispered, "I have to go to the bathroom again."

She sighed and stood up. She held out her hand. "Come on then."

He walked beside her until they got to the third gunman. "He needs to go again."

"What's his problem, he got a bladder infection or something?"

"Likely just nerves," she said quietly. The gunman moved to the side and let them pass. As the bathroom was right there, she motioned to Kevin to go in.

"No shutting the door," the gunman warned the same as he had every other time they'd been forced to come this way.

"We won't." She gave Kevin a little shove toward the bathroom. "Go on. It will be fine."

Kevin gave the gunman a worried look before racing inside. He shut the door just enough for privacy while she stood outside. She deliberately kept her gaze on the door straight ahead. She had an excellent memory, she was a hobbyist photographer after all, and she'd recognize this *type* of man anywhere. They even looked similar. They all wore khakis. They all had black hair and long beards. Each had dark eyes and larger slightly hooked noses. They all had mustaches. Their builds were similar. She didn't get it. All brothers of the same family? They were all roughly the same age. Or within ten years. And that made it possible. But...as she stole a sideways glance at the one guarding the bathroom, she realized their faces would have something unique to them. She struggled to find a way to identify the men from each other.

The man beside her smirked when he caught her looking at him.

Damn.

She didn't want him to notice her. But it was already too late. They'd been eyeing her since they'd arrived. She was casually dressed in jeans and a t-shirt with a heavy sweater over top. Decently covered but still showing too much for her peace of mind. Her stepmother was much prettier and more attractively dressed and barely a decade older. Why weren't they looking at her the same way?

Because she was the senator's daughter? She had to find a way out of this damn cabin before one of the men decided she'd make a great way to pass the time or to pressure her father into doing what they wanted. They probably didn't know that nothing would make her father change his mind.

The bathroom door opened and Kevin stumbled out. She reached for him. "My turn. Stand right here and wait for me." He nodded but his lower lip trembled. She gave him a quick hug and walked into the bathroom. She knew the guard had watched her last time, his position allowing him to see her in the mirror.

She deliberately bent so as to keep out of his view as much as possible. When done, and wow had she become fast, she quickly washed her hands and walked out to her brother. He looked horrible. Fear had turned his eyes to huge orbs. He gave a tiny shake of his head to the right. She glanced over and saw the heated gaze in the guard's eyes as it locked on her. Shit.

With her throat too seized to speak she led her brother back to the fireplace. She had to escape. These men might have done this to force her father to help them on some stupid ruling, but they had no trouble seeing her as spoils of war. She had to get through the night and was very much afraid that it wouldn't be alone.

THE TEAM HAD been silent as they trekked through the wilderness. They'd checked the coordinates several times, but no sign of the cabin yet. The wet weather wasn't helping. With nightfall coming, they had no idea if the senator and his family were going to make it until morning. There were four family members here. The senator's third and much younger wife, their eight-year-old son, plus his twenty–five year-old-daughter from marriage number two. The senator himself was in his mid–seventies.

He had a reputation as being a square man. A bit old fashioned and stuck in his ways and if his cohort's reports came in a two hundred-page style, his tomes were usually five times that. Much to the consternation of anyone forced to read it. Long-winded maybe, but often with solidly made points.

And he had a reputation for being a good man. Unswayed by popular opinion. A bit stodgy in his views maybe but he was thorough and pragmatic. Not someone who bent to pressure or could be bribed – apparently. But when a man's family was threatened, Shadow wasn't sure any man would hold out. If you wanted to maximize pressure on a person, take his family hostage. In this case, they'd taken the whole family. And that was the part that really confused Shadow.

Why? If they'd done this while the senator was home to do their bidding, they could have whisked the family anywhere in the world.

If the senator didn't survive this "holiday," it could be months before he was replaced. Or longer. It wasn't a simple process to appoint a new member to the senate.

Then why kidnap the family? Why not just kill the senator outright? He highly doubted the kidnappers had a conscience. But if so, maybe they were expecting the senator to do the right thing so they weren't forced to kill everyone. Because of course if they killed him, they'd have to kill them all. And no one wanted that.

Or was something else going on?

At a signal from Mason, they all stood up silently. Hidden under different trees they were close enough to be in contact but far enough that no one could see them all together. Cooper was closest to him. Now back to active duty, and not a moment too soon, Cooper was chomping at the bit for some serious action. He'd been sidelined with abdominal injuries that had stopped him from carrying the weight required out in the field. He'd healed but had been too overzealous and caused a setback with several pulled muscles. He bounced to his feet, appearing to be in glowing health now.

Moving in formation, Shadow leading, they hopefully were closing in on the cabin. The wind had picked up, making the going tougher. The undergrowth was wet and footing treacherous. With the dark of night settling in early, they'd need to locate the cabin and make plans when they saw the lay of the land. It was easy to make plans on paper but the terrain would have a lot to do with their next move. Shadow was completely okay to hike in and out, but he wasn't sure the senator was up to that level of physical exertion. And there was no point in saving him only to kill him on the way home.

Hat slung low over his eyes with the rain sliding off the brim to the left, he carefully assessed the way forward. Seeing the next step, he took a sharp right and picked up the pace. It couldn't be too long now.

CHAPTER 3

"ARI, I'M HUNGRY," Kevin whispered.

She hugged him little closer. "Sorry, bud. I don't know if dinner will happen."

He gave her long look. She grinned. "I know. For you that's going to be horrible."

"I haven't eaten since we got here," he exclaimed. "Surely they don't mean to starve us."

"There's food." That was the man with the cell phone. "But not what you're used to." He got up and walked to a box at the side. One of a good dozen boxes. Without any fanfare, he pulled out a jar of peanut butter and a loaf of bread. He tossed them at Kevin. "This is your dinner."

Kevin lit up. "Hey thanks."

The gunman looked at him oddly for a few moments then shrugged.

"Can I have something to spread the peanut butter?" Kevin asked in his guttural tone.

The gunman glared at him, then pulled out a plastic spoon and gave it to him.

Again the irrepressible spirit of a child on an adventure surfaced. Kevin snatched it up and opened the peanut butter. The spoon went in and he didn't bother with the bread – the first spoon went right in his mouth. If there was one food guaranteed to put a smile on Kevin's face it was peanut butter. Arianna rolled her eyes and helped him to spread peanut butter on several slices of bread. She slapped tops on both of them and handed them over to him.

He took one in each hand and had the first gone before she'd managed to make up two more. She nodded to their parents. "Go offer them some."

Still buoyed by the peanut butter, he headed to his father with a sandwich in each hand. Arianna watched as she continued making sandwiches. Her father was gruff and often distant but she knew in his own way he loved Kevin. However, he hated peanut butter.

Yet, with a resigned look on his face, the senator accepted the sandwich and whispered, "Thanks."

Kevin grinned. "I'll get you a second one too."

He turned to his mother. "Mom, do you want one?"

Arianna lowered her gaze. It was painful to see the other woman so out of her element. She'd not wanted to come in the first place, had made life for her father hellish for weeks and now seeing as what had happened, she could imagine what her stepmother was thinking.

"No, I most certainly do not." She turned on her husband. "See, I told you we shouldn't have come." She glared at him from watery eyes. "This is a terrible place."

He reached out and patted her knee. "We're here now and we'll make the best of it."

Kevin kept holding out the second sandwich to his mother.

Arianna watched, waited. Her gaze narrow, Linda stared at the sandwich like it was a viper about to strike and opened her mouth as if to offer a scathing report only to catch sight of Arianna's hard gaze. Her face pinched and she shot a glare at Arianna as if this mess was her fault, then accepted the sandwich. "Thank you, Kevin. Very kind of you."

Beaming, and seemingly unaware of the tension between the two most important women in his life, Kevin raced back to Arianna. "Two more please."

She nodded and handed him the next two sandwiches.

He reached almost instantly with empty hands. She had made four more by now. He snatched up two and walked over to the gunman who'd given him the peanut butter. "These are for you."

Silence.

Everyone in the room stared as the young boy held out the sandwiches to his captor. Arianna wanted to look around and see what the other men would do. Hell, she didn't know what this first man would do, but she hoped not beat the child for being impertinent. Instead, the gunmen accepted the sandwiches and returned to the game on his cell phone.

After that Kevin went to the other three gunmen inside the house. She worried when he went down the hallway to the kitchen and back door where the fourth man stood.

Still he came back empty handed.

Then he realized the bag was empty and his face fell. He studied the two sandwiches left in her hand. One she'd been taking bites out of as she worked. She laughed and handed over her second sandwich. "That will teach you to give all the food away while you're still hungry."

"I might be a little hungry, but better that than everyone being really hungry."

Arianna smiled. She loved her kid brother. He said the most wonderful things. She had no idea how her stepmother had created him, and he looked nothing like her father or herself so she'd always worried he might not even be genetically related but knew DNA had been checked at his birth. He was family, but it wouldn't have mattered to her one bit if he technically weren't. He was precious regardless.

They had to make it out of here. She wanted to believe they would. Her whole life functioned on an irrepressible positive good humor and outlook on life. Kevin had his whole life ahead of him. She did in theory too, but she'd do what she could to save him. She'd focus on that and work to make it happen. She didn't know what the kidnappers' plan was at this point – they'd been very sparse with their commands thus far, limiting their talking to clear orders.

As Kevin curled back up in her lap, she realized how late it was getting. She suspected there'd be no rescue this night. Unfortunately. She smiled. She'd hope for the morning.

Then the man who'd given Kevin the food said, "It's time for you to go to bed."

Kevin looked over at him, his body tense, his arm hooked around Arianna's. "The bedroom upstairs?"

The gunman nodded. "Two rooms. Two beds. You and your sister in one and your parents in the other. You first."

Thank God. Arianna hated to think that they planned to separate her from her brother, but with the looks they'd been giving her, she'd been worried. She got to her feet, knowing they'd be escorted. There was a bathroom up there as well. With one man behind her and her brother, they climbed the stairs to the bedroom.

Every step she worried the next would be her last. Her dad and Linda stayed below. They still needed her father for something. She hoped. Kevin gripped her hand so tight she knew he was terrified. Upstairs, their bags already in their room, they quickly grabbed up their toothbrushes and went to the bathroom. The gunman never left. Kevin didn't want to go to the bathroom while the man watched. She half covered him and persuaded him to get the job done then they could get into bed. Awkwardly, he finished and washed up his hands. Now it was her turn.

Kevin turned his back and stared at the gunman as if willing him to take him on. Then he crossed his arms and spread his legs in defiance.

The gunman laughed. But the trick worked. By the time the gunman's gaze had shifted back to her, she'd already finished and had approached the sink to wash her hands. In the mirror she caught sight of his disappointment. He was just pure slime.

In the bedroom the gunman had closed and locked the door. She hadn't even realized there was a lock on it, not remembering it being there last time. In fact, the knob was very new looking.

As in this had been preplanned and all contingencies worked out.

Then she heard raised voices downstairs and realized they were going to work her father over while they were forced to listen upstairs. She had to distract Kevin. He'd heard enough already.

Damn.

THE CABIN NESTLED deep inside the trees below. Shadow

walked out on a ledge overlooking the tranquil setting.

Or what could be a tranquil scene if a storm wasn't blasting through the area covering them in rain and blowing branches into their faces. Still, there were lights on inside and that gave it a look of a haven from the storm. His team were spread out, taking up positions. They had work to do before going in on a blind rescue. As of now they didn't know how many men were here and if the hostages were even still alive. His radio crackled lightly. He adjusted the sound, listening to the conversation going on around him.

One man on east corner. Assault rifle over the shoulder. Two hand guns.

Shadow's lips turned down at the corner. The men were loaded for bear.

Grenades on a clip at his back.

Shit. Most kidnappers weren't equipped with grenades.

The radio sounded again. This time it was Dane talking. "Unit is a half mile out. Will be coming on foot from here."

The team traveling cross-country had arrived on schedule. Now to figure out how many terrorists they were up against – and to confirm that the hostages were still alive. It would be easy enough to pick off the one man outside but not until they were ready to move. Or the hostages would be sacrificed.

Second man on the southwest corner, came the low whisper. Mason.

That was two outside guards identified. Shadow studied the cabin. One single front door at the top of four stairs. A large lazy porch wrapping from the front to the left side. The windows long and low. So no traveling from one side to the other without being seen. He continued to catalog the house. Noting the light on upstairs on the right and the lights on in the main living room. Smoke curled lazily from the chimney. If they hadn't had the text from the daughter and seen the two guards, no one else would have any idea something was wrong.

But he knew.

The woods were alive with tension.

Upstairs a woman moved to the window and stared out. The daughter, Arianna. Long blonde ringlets, fully dressed, arms crossed as she stared out into the world. He pulled up his binoculars to see her tapping her fingers impatiently on her arm. Her mouth pinched with tension. A young boy arrived at her side. She took him in her arms and hugged him close.

That was the senator's son, Kevin.

So the two siblings were likely locked upstairs. Were the senator and his wife up there as well? He doubted it. The terrorists were "talking" to the senator now. Not good. The senator was known to be stubborn as shit and would take the beating, but at his age, that could be lethal.

He shifted his position slightly and set his sights back on the daughter upstairs. And gazed directly in her eyes.

She stared back at him.

Surely she couldn't see him. Her gaze narrowed and tingles slid down his back. He estimated the distance between them and realized that he could see her without the binoculars so in effect she might be able to see him, but not likely… She was in the light and looking into the dark. Still…

He raised a hand to her.

She froze. And damn if she didn't slowly raise a hand casually behind the boy's back and hold it palm forward.

Excitement drove through him. Was this possible?

Then she did something with her fingers. And repeated it over and over again. He locked the binoculars on her hand movement.

She was signaling for help using signals for the deaf. And then he remembered the senator's son had several disabilities.

Whether she understood what she was seeing or not, she'd sensed someone out here. Damn. Now how could he get a message to her?

He signaled right back, *Help is here. Sit tight.* And repeated it over and over. Inside he knew she couldn't see it. Damn it. He was too far away. And what benefit would it do to find a better location.

She continued to signal until the boy leaned his head back to her. And she smiled down at him and cuddled him close. Shadow glanced down at the binoculars in his hands. He'd been given a glimpse into her personality that he'd not seen in too many other people – if any. She really loved that boy. She was the sister, not the mother, although from what he'd just seen she could have been. The bond was that strong.

There'd been something so damn caring, loving between them, he felt...and the words eluded him as he glanced at the woods around him, the rain dripping from the leaves, the moon hidden high above. He knew exactly how the boy felt. How he always felt. Alone. On the outside. Not included. This setting only amplified that feeling.

Except for one very important point. He was not a young boy any longer. He was a Navy SEAL. This was his life, and if he didn't like it he could change it. But he wasn't prepared to change very much. He'd become comfortable with his life. Understood it. Knew how it worked. So even though there were other things out there for other people, he was good with who he was and the way he was.

As he returned his gaze to the window, he realized the room had gone dark.

Just then, his radio squawked.

Senator is in the living room. Two men working him over. Wife on the floor. Condition unknown.

And he realized something else. He was who he was and that was a damn good thing for the senator's son and daughter. Because of who he was, they'd get to continue being who they were.

He'd caught sight of an escape hatch for the kids. Saving the senator was a whole different story. But if they could get the brother and sister out it removed two pawns in the game.

He quietly told his team what he was going to do.

CHAPTER 4

S HE SWORE SHE'D seen someone on the hillside across from them. She knew it was likely to be her imagination, hope creating images where there were none because she was desperate for escape.

Her father's cries below had stopped. There was only the odd moan now. And that terrified her even more. She'd turned down the hearing aids in Kevin's ears. There was no way he needed to hear his father's last cries. She was so angry but knew she had to keep Kevin safe. Even if she could charge downstairs to save her father, she'd get a bullet. That might still be a kindness when compared to the possible outcome waiting for them. But she damned well hoped not. And she'd be no help to Kevin then.

She's been signaling off and on since they'd been locked in the bedroom. Hoping against hope that someone would come. Then she thought there had been an odd flash on the hillside and a weird awareness came over her, that feeling of being stared at.

Time was running out. The kidnappers had provisions for several days from what she could see, but she had no intention of being here with them. She'd been assessing options since they'd arrived. Being on the second floor with no balcony she knew it was a hell of a long drop to the ground. She might be able to tie the sheets and blankets together to lower them enough to jump the rest of the way but getting lost in the middle of the woods wasn't exactly an answer.

But it might be the only one available. If she could evade the guards outside. She'd seen them change out the guard every hour. What she didn't know was if they were stationed outside or if they were doing rounds on the property to keep moving and cover the cabin from all angles. She'd been staring outside since forever but hadn't seen any of them. That didn't mean they weren't there. She'd been looking with the light off for the last twenty minutes. After her father had gone silent. She didn't want them to think she was awake and listening in. Better to be oblivious.

She knew the chances of her father surviving this was poor, and grief clutched at her heart. She had no idea what they'd do to Linda either. The future looked like shit for all of them. She was loathe to run and leave the two of them behind, but if it meant saving Kevin...

She'd do it in a heartbeat.

She quietly tugged the window open. And stuck her head out.

When there were no yells or shouts for her to get back inside, she leaned out further.

And jumped back out of sight as a guard walked past.

Kevin clutched at her, fear twisting his delicate features.

She held her fingers to her lips to warn him to be quiet and leaned out again, looking for the man she thought she saw. There was no sign of anyone.

As she studied the height from the ground and mentally calculated the distance the sheets would hang she realized they were directly over the living room. If they dropped down to the ground here, they'd be seen.

Shit.

There were no balconies. There were no sloping roofs to clamber across to the left or right. There was nothing helpful in that way at all. Huge trees rose beside the cabin and the branches higher up offered safety, but she had no way to get to them. The sheets were their only chance. Maybe if they were lucky they'd escape into the woods before being caught.

She slowly led Kevin back to the bed, her mind spinning but coming up empty. Kevin was counting on her. And fear was kicking in. Jesus. If the men killed their parents she and Kevin would have no chance. They were liabilities at that point. The kidnappers might try to use them for leverage, but her father had told her often he would never give in to extortion. If her father wouldn't do what he could to save them, then no one else could be bothered either.

Footsteps climbed the stairs. She closed her eyes in terror. *Oh God. Please not. Dear God. Help.*

Kevin dragged her down to the bed.

"Pretend to be asleep," she whispered.

It was as good a plan as any. Only it wasn't going to do the job. She knew that. But there weren't many options. She dare not strip the bed right now if someone was coming to check on them. But if they got a chance to leave after this asshole left, then they would.

Lying on the bed, on her stomach, hair across her face so he couldn't see her features well in the dark, she waited for the guard to come in. She briefly considered trying to kill him, but how. With what?

It wasn't possible – was it?

She swallowed when she heard a hand on the knob.

Then the key turned in the lock. With Kevin frozen and tucked up to her side, she lay quiet as the door opened, letting a sliver of light enter the room. The guard stood at the doorway and studied them. She kept her hand lax on Kevin's back and her breathing slow and steady.

If anyone touched them they'd know that the two of them were tense, muscles rigid.

The guard walked to the window where she'd been looking out. And she realized her one attempt to stick her head out had been seen. As she'd seen the guard, he'd seen her. Now someone had been sent to check.

God damn it.

She should have been more careful.

The guard looked down on the ground outside and studied the window and the view outside for a long moment then spun on his heels. And walked to the bed.

She lay so damn quiet, then realized it was too quiet. She made a snuffling sound and shifted slightly. They were lying fully dressed on the covers.

He stood and stared at her for a long moment. She could hear his breathing. Sense his interest.

Her skin crawled.

Then he reached down and touched her. His fingers sliding the hair back off her face.

She sighed and moved her head on the pillow as if something disturbed her and he stepped back.

After another long moment he walked through the door and closed it. When she heard the lock click inside she slowly opened her eyes, afraid that somehow two men had come in and one might be still there waiting for her to show she'd been faking it. When the footsteps continued downstairs, she sat up and got to work. It might not be the best idea but it was all she had.

They couldn't stay here.

IT TOOK PRECIOUS time to get into position. Even then he was thinking this was more foolhardy venture than good idea. But he did over the top rescues and this appeared to be yet one more. The reports coming in were rough. And they had to save who they could while they could. The minute the terrorists understood they had company, the hostages were going to be killed. If they'd killed the senator and his wife already, then there was no hope for the younger two members of the family. He had to get them out now.

Using the ropes from his pack and being a decent judge of distance, he'd climbed out on a low limb, but hopefully one still strong enough to hold the weight, and after tying several knots in the rope he lowered it down to the height of the window of the bedroom where he'd seen the brother and sister.

As there was no one in the window now to see his rope, he swung it gently forward to come up and lightly tap the glass. He knew his team was watching his progress.

The first swing fell short, the second was almost there. The third hit. A heavy enough thud, and he immediately pulled it up in case someone else heard it.

After a few moments, and lying full length on the large tree limb above, he swung it again. And it tapped the window lightly. Then he did it again. And again.

Damn it, where were they?

Afraid the two had been moved he tried one more time and watched as two pale faces appeared. Arianna wasted no time. She opened the window, did something to the brother and lifted him up to the windowsill. When Shadow swung the rope toward them, she grabbed it and had the boy grab high enough up the rope that he could stand on the knot below. Then she gave him a quick kiss and swung him out and away. She stepped back out of sight but he knew she could still see the boy as he hung on for dear life. Shadow carefully hauled him up. The boy was a lightweight. But it was still dangerous getting off the rope and over the main trunk of the tree where he wrapped the boy's arms around the trunk and whispered against his ear, "Hold on. I'll be right back. I have to get your sister."

Shadow returned with the rope to where the window was still open...and the young woman waited for him.

She peered out at him then darted back, slowly lowering the window again. What was she doing? Then he watched the guard on sentry duty cross the property line, his gaze automatically going to the bedroom window.

Shadow smiled in appreciation. He could kill the guard from where he was positioned and would love to – but only once he had the girl out and safe.

She needed to be rescued too.

He waited for the sentry to pass under him and go around the house, then slowly lowered the rope. This time when he swung it to the window he found her sitting on the ledge, legs out as if to jump. She stood up awkwardly, grabbed the rope as high as she could, and then pushed the window down behind her as she let go to swing out on the rope.

Smart.

He was liking her more and more already. She climbed up that rope like a monkey and as she made her way to where he was lying silently, he couldn't help but admire her. She was almost eye level, her gaze busy as she looked for a way to get up onto the tree. When he extended his arm, she reached up and clasped his forearm. He sat up and tugged, she landed in his arms. Very nice.

She lay there trembling for a long moment then turned to look directly at him. For a long moment their gazes locked. Then she said, "It was you, on the hill, wasn't it?"

He nodded. "Yes," he whispered. "Need to get the rope out of sight. Kevin is back at the main trunk."

She caught sight of her brother, carefully gained her footing and made her way over to him. Shadow, his hands busy pulling up his rope, looped it properly then stuffed it in his pack. He was surprised to see both Kevin and Arianna had backpacks with them. It was good but it had taken a presence of mind he hadn't expected.

He approached and with an arm around both of them he explained who he was and what they were going to do next.

Neither said a word until he was done. Then Kevin reached out and grabbed his hand, whispered in a hard to understand guttural voice, "Thank you."

CHAPTER 5

S EALS. OH THANK God. Even though she was still out in the middle of the wilderness with the terrorists down below holding her family captive, having SEALs here was a game changer. A big one. Still, they were a long way from being safe. Too early to celebrate. And then there was her father...

"The guard just checked on us. So our disappearance might not be noticed for a while, I don't know how often they will check."

"Right. Let's get you out of here," Shadow said.

Kevin froze. "Daddy?"

"We're going after them but that's for us to do. Not you."

"Do you want us to stay here until you come back?" she asked, looking around. They had to be a good thirty feet up in the air. They couldn't be seen from the ground and they were out of the rain. "This works. We're hidden and safe. We can settle on these big limbs until you get back."

"No, we should get further away. Stray bullets and all that."

She studied his lean face as he searched and assessed the area below them. His radio buzzed several times as the men communicated plans with each other. Suddenly there was some activity down below. Two men came out of the house and converged on the one guard who'd come back around again on his next pass.

Raised voices and agitated movements said something bad had happened, but she had no idea what. She watched the SEAL as he studied what was going on.

Then a light came on in her bedroom.

"Shit."

That had been their window of escape. "How did they know?" she muttered in a low voice.

"It doesn't matter. They probably are checking on a regular basis anyway or maybe they saw something..." He surged forward to watch the men scurry out of the house and spread wide. "This is a good thing."

Immediately there were several pings and the one man deepest in the woods went down without a sound. From where she sat she could see another soldier in heavy combat gear step out from behind a tree and though the terrorists were big, this man was huge. He approached the terrorist from behind, and she didn't see what happened next but she could imagine. The SEAL shifted the man's body until it was hidden in the bush. So simple. So easy. For him.

They had a perfect view in front and below where they perched, but for the tree branches, couldn't see in other directions at all. So she had no idea what else was happening with the other men that had been inside. Surely they wouldn't have all come out on the one side of the house. That made no sense. But then maybe they had more men than she knew about. There were sounds of a powerful engine arriving. She glanced at her rescuer. "Is that yours?"

He shook his head. "Sounds like reinforcements to move you to a new location."

"Glad we're out of there then," she said with feeling. But

there wasn't the same joy for their parents. She watched as both were escorted out of the cabin. Relieved to see both walking, although bent over and holding onto each other as they were prodded into the new truck, she was also dismayed to see so many new soldiers exiting out the back of the vehicle. This was not good. It appeared they'd brought another eight, possibly ten men. Why would they need so many? And these were dressed in the same khakis again. That made them easier to spot and easy to tell apart from the SEALs. Then again she couldn't see the SEALs. She had no idea where they were or how many were here. She glanced over at the man at her side, but he was studying three men sneaking up on a clump of brush to the side. She wondered what they thought could possibly be there when the SEAL beside her did a quick tie of the rope around the branch he stood on and dropped.

As in straight down.

On top of the first man and wiped out the second before a SEAL hidden in the bushes took out the third.

"Wow," she whispered.

Kevin beamed at her. "Yeah, he's awesome."

She'd never seen anything like it. Who could unless they did this kind of training? It was not something she ever wanted to experience again but the way this man moved, so graceful and yet wild, untamed. And he was so damn silent.

Looking down below them again she studied the ground looking for *her* SEAL. And couldn't find him. She shifted to glance at other areas through the trees but there was no sign of him. She wished she'd asked his name.

"Where did he go?" she asked Kevin in a hoarse voice.

He stared down below. "I don't know. He

just…disappeared."

With no incentive to leave the safety of their hiding place, the two hunkered down to wait. They watched the ground intently believing that their rescuer might return any moment. But nothing happened for at least an hour and by then she'd started to worry. What if he couldn't come back for them? He was only one man. Big and strong and obviously damn capable, but still, just a flesh and blood human like all the dead men down below.

Not that she could see any of them.

The vehicles were still parked outside the house, and their parents were still seated inside the back of the newest one. She studied the truck. It was a foolish thought but what if she could get into the driver's side… Could she drive out and get them to safety?

Had any of the men gone to guard inside the vehicle with her dad and Linda? Not likely as they weren't a threat anymore. Did the terrorists even understand that there was a bigger threat than themselves around here? Were they looking for her and her brother? Or were they going to assume the worst. Without the bodies of their fallen comrades that should throw them into confusion as to exactly what had happened. She'd rewound the SEAL's rope so no one else would know they were up here but as she stared at it, still tied to the limb they were sitting on, she couldn't help but wonder if there was something more she could do. More she *should* do.

Kevin made an odd gurgling sound. She studied his face, fatigue had bleached the color from his skin. Did he need his medicine? The shocks had happened so fast they had to be hard for him to deal with. She wasn't even sure what all his medications were for as his mother handled all that. But although he was looking tired, what he needed more than anything was to know he was safe and to see his parents again.

She didn't know about the last one. She hoped they'd survive but was loathe to put Kevin in any danger. They were safe here. They needed to stay.

And that rope in her arms could stay right there too.

"HOW ARE THE kids?"

Shadow stared at Swede. "The boy is a kid but the daughter is twenty–five. Nothing kiddish about her."

Swede's huge grin split his face. Typical. Always a smile no matter what. But when you needed him, he was all business. He was a good man to have at your back. They all were. Cooper slid over to join them, Markus and Evan at his side.

"The senator and his wife are in the truck. No guards."

"Do we know that for sure?" Markus motioned in a low voice. "I can't see leaving the prisoners without a guard."

"Unless there are no prisoners," Evan said in a sarcastic tone. "A sleight of hand maybe?"

Shadow frowned. Why would they do that? The senator needed medical aid and wasn't likely in any shape to escape so they didn't need guards, but surely the terrorists had figured out that they were under attack by now. And stealing the truck was also a possibility.

He shifted position to get a better view of the confab raging inside the kitchen. He said, "All the hostages are outside. The terrorists are inside. We need to go in and take them down now."

Mason's voice came over the radio, low and clear. They were

going in.

Shadow muttered back, "Is someone guarding the senator?" A short time later, Mason came back. "Two guards down. They were assigned to guard the truck."

Shadow confirmed he'd grab the truck with the senator and slipped between the trees. He was concerned that someone hidden was going to be looking out for the victims. But there were no drivers inside and no passengers. So just the senator and his wife. Unless there was a gunman hidden inside waiting. He took several steps forward until an odd sound registered. He stepped back and was tackled from behind.

He spun and grabbed and twisted his attacker to the ground and realized his hands were grabbing soft flesh, soft material, and there was nothing enemy like about the beautiful worried face beneath him. Arianna.

He reared back in shock, his mind trying to process what she was doing, when she whispered, "You can't touch the truck. We saw someone plant a device underneath. Looked like dynamite." Her voice was hoarse but defiant.

He didn't know what to say. He quickly withdrew and dragged her with him back into hiding. "Tell me again exactly what you saw," he said. His mind struggled at the idea that she'd left her brother up in the tree to come and save him. He had never expected such a thing and didn't know what to do with the information now.

She quickly related what she'd seen and her gut decision to drop down and save him. He stared at her again. "And your brother?"

"He's safe," she whispered, "He was in agreement."

He wanted to ask why but knew he couldn't. She explained

anyway. "We couldn't let you be killed when you'd saved us. Besides we need you to help save our parents." Her grin flashed.

"It's my job to save," he said in low tones, turning his gaze to search their surroundings while he tried to process the information.

"And it's my job to save you when I could. Anyone would have in the same situation," she retorted. "You're welcome by the way."

And damn if she didn't reach up and kiss him.

Once again thunderstruck by her actions, his hand instinctively slapped his cheek where she'd kissed him. And he blinked at her in shock.

She grinned and reached up and kissed his other cheek.

He lifted his other hand to slap his other cheek then narrowed his gaze as he realized how silly he looked.

Then she pulled his head down and laid one on him. He couldn't help but respond. She demanded a response. One he couldn't hold back.

"Harrumph."

She broke away and spun to stare up. As in way up. Swede. Her gaze widened and she plastered back against Shadow. Shadow knew there'd be no end to ribbing now. He glared at the huge smirking Swede who was flanked by a wildly grinning Cooper. Behind were Markus and Evan with grins on their faces as well. Everyone at base had heard about their group's love matches. Hell, they were likely the laughing stock of SEALs everywhere. Unless you were jealous…

Several guys had asked to join their ranks on the next mission. Half joking but some were very serious. The type of work they did, it was tough on relationships and now that so many of his friends had seemed to find a magic formula the other guys wanted in.

"Thank you very much for saving my dear friend, Shadow here," Swede said in a gentle voice. "Don't mind him if his manners are a little rusty." And that smile of his that melted hearts everywhere appeared to melt Arianna's too. Still lying flat against him, she held out her hand and said, "At least now I know his name."

She twisted to grin up at Shadow. "And it's okay if his manners are a little rusty. His skills in other areas obviously…aren't."

And damn it, heat rose to this face. He had no idea who this woman was but he was…interested…intrigued. Hell, he was…no, he refused to admit it. Attraction was one thing. But this…whatever this was…had to be something else again.

Cooper stepped behind Shadow and chanted, "Another one bites the dust."

CHAPTER 6

ARIANNA COULDN'T STOP touching him. She was a toucher by nature, but when she'd seen the man who'd rescued her and her brother head toward the truck and knew he had seconds to live, she'd used the rope like he had and swung out and let go. And had landed on him. It had worked a little too well maybe, but she was down and he was fine.

And damn it, she ran her fingers over his features yet again, he felt so good.

"I'm fine," Shadow muttered, pulling her hands down.

The other SEALs had huge grins on their faces. She'd heard them called Swede, Cooper, Markus and Evan. What was it about the SEALs that made them all dashing and dangerous looking? She studied them. Swede was a blonde mountain, Cooper was only slightly smaller. Markus was dark, swarthy. Evan was the opposite, so blond his hair appeared almost white. Not to mention sexy. At that she turned to look back at Shadow, her mind immediately adding *very sexy...*

Shadow, and what kind of name was that, didn't appear to know what to do with her.

Hell, she didn't know what to do with her. He set her on her feet and turned to face the truck, his face leaning out as he considered the problem. "Swede, weight sensitive do you think?"

"I'm thinking so. Cooper, Evan, what do you think?"

"It would make sense but that's going to have been made here. Too touchy for that kind of travel." Evan said.

Cooper nodded but stayed silent.

"But they'd have been able to travel with the unit mostly built then add the mechanism here if that was the case," Arianna said absentmindedly. "They brought no equipment that I could see."

The group stared at her. "What? If I didn't see any bombs or bomb making equipment, then they likely brought it here with the truck." She spun back to look at it. "I wonder if the truck is stolen. Destroy it in the Canadian wilderness and leave it behind. A good way to make sure it's never found."

With Shadow still studying her, she turned warm under that intense light in his eyes. If he'd been confused before he was even more so now. She smiled up at him. "It's a hobby."

"Bomb making," he asked carefully, his gaze narrow.

She laughed. "No, mysteries."

With a confused look on all their faces, she explained. "I'm a mystery buff. Go to mystery dinners, read the latest and the best, not to mention every other one I can get my hands on."

"Cool," Cooper said. "That always appealed."

She turned to see Shadow's reaction, noting the dark gaze before it was turned back to face the truck that held her dad and stepmom. She wanted to call out but didn't dare bring any unwanted attention. She glanced upward to see her brother staring down at her. She waved.

He grinned.

Her hand was lowered and she was jerked back behind Shadow. She frowned at him. He glared at her. And she realized she'd completely forgotten that there were other men out here still and she wasn't safe.

She was an innocent, but he was keeping her safe.

She beamed at him.

His gaze narrowed on her then shifted to look at his buddies. Arianna caught the other men hastily hiding grins.

"Aren't you going to diffuse the bomb?" she asked. "Anytime now would be good."

Shadow's eyebrows shot up to the hairline. But he stayed quiet – just shook his head.

"I'll check it out," Cooper said. Shadow moved the group back, keeping Arianna behind him and Swede. Markus and Evan split away and headed off to sides.

She snuck up closer until she was plastered against the huge tree beside them as the men kept watch for Cooper.

Cooper slid over to the vehicle and lay down. He reached up and she gasped, her hand instinctively grasping Shadow's hand. Gunfire rained down around them. She cried out and covered her head.

Then suddenly Cooper was out from under the vehicle and racing toward them.

He joined them crouched in the bush. "Simple enough. No timer. No pressure sensitivity. Likely remote detonation just in case we did drive the truck away with the senator."

She squeezed Shadow's hand. "He's good."

When Shadow didn't say anything, she gave his hand a shake. "Isn't he?"

Shadow slanted a look her way. "They are all good."

She beamed. "See. Shadow thinks you're good too."

Cooper, his eyes dancing, said to Shadow, "Thanks, buddy.

Your opinion means a lot to me."

With a snort, Shadow disengaged his hand and disappeared into the woods. Just like that.

"Where did he go?" she asked after several long moments searching the woods around her.

"He did what he does best, walks in the shadows."

"Hence his name." She nodded. "Did any of you consider that he does that because he's always alone? Thinks he's always going to be alone," she added in exasperation. "That's not a good thing you know."

Swede stared at her, a peculiar look in his eyes and said gently, "He'll continue to believe that until someone comes along and changes it for him."

Then he disappeared in the bushes too.

Cooper smiled down at her. "It's nice to see you already understand Shadow."

"I don't know that I understand him," she cautioned. "He saved my life."

"And you saved his," he said cheerfully. "Isn't there something to that old adage about saving a life and being responsible for that life ever after?"

"Then our scales would just cross each other's off as we're even," she said a little reluctantly, intrigued at the idea of having a man like Shadow feel a little responsible for her. Not totally responsible because that would feel like a ball and chain over time, and she couldn't handle shackles. Still...he was...all man. Sigh.

"Not at all. It would mean that he is to look after you, but that you are also to look after him."

"We're so different, that would hardly work," she said with a smile, speaking in light tones. Too bad Shadow wasn't still here.

"Oh, but you'd be caretakers of different parts of each other. Like you could look after the part of him that feels alone. Empty," Cooper added quietly. "Shadow needs to know that he has someone in his life besides his brothers." He tapped his chest. "He and the rest of our team."

"Doesn't he have any family?" It would be tough to be all alone. She didn't like her stepmother, had learned to deal with her gruff father, but she'd be lost without Kevin.

Cooper shook his head. "And he's very private."

She nodded, staring into the bushes. "Poor man."

"I don't think sympathy is on the menu."

"No, neither is pity. He doesn't need it either. He's survived and that's the best any of us can do sometimes." She tilted her head back to see the rope too high up for her to reach. "I need to get back up to my brother." She turned to Cooper. "Can you give me a boost up?"

The words weren't fully out of her mouth before she was literally tossed up into the air in the direction of the rope. She grabbed on and scurried up to where her brother sat anxiously waiting for her.

Her arms were aching, and her breathing uneven by the time she got to the top. But she made it, and with her brother tucked up close in her arms, the two of them safe against the trunk, and the rope once again looped around the branch, she closed her eyes and rested.

Shadow…an interesting name for an interesting man.

SHADOW STUDIED THE four men in front. They weren't as well

trained as the other soldiers and stood talking as a group. Then he realized that his group hadn't been much better. And that was disheartening. Trust a woman to create such a situation. Hell, before she'd arrived he'd been doing well. Now he was scattered and confused. He shoved all thoughts of Arianna back inside. She was a job. That was all.

Liar.

But he wouldn't listen.

Swede joined him. Markus on his heels. Shadow glanced behind.

"She's with Cooper."

Shadow nodded but the thought soured his gut. Great. The only other single guy in the unit and one who was friendly and got along wonderfully with everyone. Wait, Markus and Evan were here too. Great. More men for her to choose from. Yet he shouldn't give a damn. She was nothing to do with him. Good for Cooper if he found someone. He'd had a shitty year. Then Markus deserved a relationship after losing his wife. And what about Evan's divorce? He could use a sweetheart himself. Someone like Arianna would be perfect.

And that made his stomach want to heave.

Suddenly the enemy in front of him were on the move, two to the left and two to the right. He headed right, Swede beside him. Markus walked the center line.

The two men went down without a fight. Shadow stared at an unconscious man at his feet. He quickly secured him and turned to see Swede already lifting the other over his shoulder.

They were collecting the men and keeping them on the other side of the hill under heavy guard. So far they'd managed to take several out without alerting the enemy.

But then the men had been easy to capture. And he wondered about that. As in they were *too* easy to capture. Shouldn't these men be more of a challenge?

Swede leaned closer. "Canadian team is suspicious. Says it's too easy."

"I agree." Shadow studied the collection of soldiers. "They don't look worried."

"We've disarmed them," Markus said adding, "at least our weapons stash is growing."

Then Shadow got it. He spun around behind him, searching for the enemy. "They are a distraction. While we're here worrying about them, the others are setting plans in motion."

"Time to get back to the cabin." Swede pivoted and blended into the woods. Shadow was close enough behind to hear his radio crackle and Mason's voice but too far behind to hear the words. He suspected they were all considering what was beneath this ploy.

"We need to make sure the senator is okay," he muttered to Mason.

"He's still in the truck."

"I'm not sure he is." Markus shook his head. "Like I said before, I think that's a slight of hand movement and we fell for it."

There was an awkward silence on the other end. "That would not be good."

Swede, slightly ahead, turned and nodded in agreement at Shadow. There had to be some reason for the extra men to be scattered and easily caught.

Not to mention they were well trained soldiers. They were trained killers, weapons aside.

The truck came into view.

And lying underneath, trying to do something, was Cooper again. This time he had Evan helping him.

Then where the hell was Arianna? He spun and twisted so he could peer up into the trees above then shifted to look at others around him lest the enemy could see him and understand what he'd been looking for. He'd caught sight of Kevin's black windbreaker. Enough to know the boy was up there.

Cooper motioned to him with his hand. Shadow crouched down to see what the issue was. And found a second bomb. Jesus. He ran fingers over his face.

Just as he was trying to figure what to do, bullets circled the truck in a hail of gunfire, all coming from high up in the trees.

They were surrounded.

Shadow melted into the background. He hated to leave Cooper under the truck. If anyone chose to shoot the truck then the hostages, if they were still there, Cooper would be killed. That's why they hadn't had a guard down below. The guards had been above.

And that meant Kevin and Arianna were in trouble too. He spun in time to see Swede take aim and fire. A man gave a cry and fell to the ground twenty feet away. He landed heavy and didn't move.

Instantly, the area where they stood came under a barrage of bullets. But they'd moved already. Swede popped off another one as Shadow raced to the base of the tree holding the two family members. Gunfire spat all around him.

Realizing they'd been outplayed, he scrambled up the tree as Swede moved in and out of the bushes below him drawing the fire away.

In the distance he heard more gunshots. Not a good sign. Their captives had probably heard the gunfire and used it as a signal to overpower the men guarding them. The Canadian contingency had been right. This was too easy. Well, not any longer. Shadow climbed rapidly. He landed quietly on the huge branch he'd left Kevin on and found him wrapped around the tree, his eyes closed and trembling.

"Kevin, it's me," Shadow whispered.

Kevin's eyes popped open and he stared at Shadow. Then threw himself into his arms. Unprepared for the onslaught, Shadow had to quickly adjust his grip and position to handle the tiny tornado. But he held him close to his chest. "Where is your sister?" he asked, quietly searching through the tree. She'd been left with Cooper. Cooper was under the truck. He gave Kevin a shake. "Where is your sister?"

"Don't know." Kevin lifted a tear stained face to him. "She saw someone on another tree trying to make their way over here. She told me to stay here and she took off."

Damn, that means Cooper had helped her return to her brother then had gone to check out the truck. But if she'd stayed down below then chances were good that Kevin would have been spirited away without anyone the wiser. Holding Kevin tight to his chest, he searched through the branches.

And saw her crouching on a branch, the back of her clothing blending in with the greenery around her.

On a branch above her stood a soldier.

His heart pounded as he realized the soldier hadn't seen her. He turned and looked down at something. Shadow followed his gaze and caught sight of Swede moving through the trees. Shadow pulled out his gun and lined it up, but it was hard to get a good shot. As he waited for the right moment, Arianna rose up from her crouched position and with a large branch hit the soldier at the back of the knees. He cried out, toppled over, tried to save himself but she whacked him a second time and he fell.

Nice.

Arianna stared over the edge at her handiwork and then as if realizing she'd taken out one but there could be scores more she needed to watch out for, she spun around, ducking deeper out of sight. As that gaze of hers swung back toward Kevin, it landed on Shadow.

Shadow grinned.

She gave him a slow smile that seemed to light up the darkness around them. Then she glanced past to check for more soldiers before zinging back in his direction. She shifted her attention, finding a path back toward them. Shadow kept an eye on her progress while trying to keep her safe from other shooters. But silence had fallen. Everywhere.

They were all in a state of waiting. For someone to make a mistake.

Arianna managed to make it to the tree next to him. She reached out to step over to another branch.

A single shot fired.

Arianna cried out and stumbled. She grabbed a branch and hung on.

Several more shots were fired and a lone gunmen fell from the tree.

Kevin called, "Arianna?"

Shadow pulled him back out of the way in case anyone else heard him. But there was no corresponding gunfire. His gaze tracked Arianna who was still standing but trembling. "You need to stay here and don't make a sound," he said to Kevin and left the boy hugging the tree.

Shadow quickly slipped through the boughs and made it to Arianna's side. He ran his hands over her body until he came to stickiness on her thigh. Crouching low he bent and checked out the wound. The bullet had gone in and through the top of her thigh. Painful as all hell but could be so much worse. He had to go by touch alone given the endless blackness around them.

Tiny whimpers sounded through her mouth as she tried to hold them back. Shock was the issue now. He pulled out his knife and cut the bottom of her t–shirt from under her sweater and quickly bound up the wound. Then wrapping an arm around her, he half carried her half supported her as they slowly made their way back to her brother.

"I'd really like to go home now," she whispered against his neck. "I'll never look at tree climbing the same way again."

"Too bad as you do it so well."

She gave a broken gurgle of a laugh. "No, I don't. Or I wouldn't have gotten shot."

"Ah, you see that's because you weren't supposed to play cops and robbers at the same time."

She gave a half snort that for some stupid reason he found wonderful. Back at her brother, he slowly lowered her until she was sitting on the thick branch. It was pitch black outside but the rain had slowed. "Any chance we can move back into the house," she said, her teeth chattering. "I'm starting to wish I'd never left."

Kevin wrapped his arms around her as if to keep her warm. "Don't say that, Ari, you know what they were going to do to you."

At the boy's words, Shadow swiveled to look at Arianna's

face. She looked miserable, wet now, but she held Kevin close. Not wanting to ask for an explanation for Kevin's statement, he looked at Arianna, one eyebrow raised. She shrugged then nodded.

Damn. He hadn't really considered that. This kidnapping had a political overtone, but she was a beautiful young woman and rape was often meted out as a punishment and to control the victims. He was glad she'd made it out first.

"I'm fine, Kevin. Sorry for whining."

Whining? That wasn't close to being a whine but as long as she had Kevin to keep bolstered she'd do her best. And he respected that.

Down below nothing stirred. Off to the side he heard a long drawn out hawk's cry. He quickly cupped his hand and gave a corresponding cry. He looped the rope back over his arm and studied the pair. "I'm going to carry Kevin down on my back. Then I'm going to come back up for you, Arianna, okay?"

"No, I don't want to leave her," Kevin cried.

"Hush, Kevin," she said, her voice soothing. "This will be fine. I'm safe here."

Swede came out from the bushes and held up his arms. Shadow tied the rope around Kevin's waist and dropped him down into Swede's waiting arms. Then with Arianna clinging to his back, he carefully climbed down the tree. When on solid ground, he helped her stand on her own feet. The color drained out of her face, she barely held back the cry of pain when she tried to put weight on her injured leg.

Before she could collapse, he swung her up into his arms and carried her back to the camp where they'd held the rebels with Swede at his side carrying Kevin. She looped her arms around his neck and snuggled in damn near breaking his heart. She shouldn't be so trusting. The world was full of assholes.

Cooper, now out from under the truck, raced after them. "I think I've got it dismantled. I need help though."

"I'm here." Hawk slid out from behind a tree. Evan shifted to guard the direction he came from then disappeared from sight. "Dane is at the camp and Mason is on his way. Evan is heading back. What do you need?"

"I think I can get the senator out from the back of the truck now. But I don't want the rebels to know that we have them."

Arianna tilted her head upwards and whispered, "Go help. I'm fine."

"You're not fine," he said shortly but his attention followed the others. "They should have someone to watch out for them."

She gave him a push on the shoulder. "Put me down," she said. "Swede, leave Kevin here with me."

"No, ma'am."

"Yes. Those are our parents and we don't even know if they survived that beating. Save them," she ordered. "Kevin is fine with me. You'll only be gone a few minutes anyway." And she gave him a sharp nod as if to underscore the right actions for him to follow.

Swede grinned, glanced at Shadow, and said, "I think we've been told."

"She doesn't understand," Shadow said. "We have to get her and her brother to safety."

"And you have, several times, in fact, so far this night. Now get our parents and maybe we can all get the hell out of here."

She tilted her chin at him and narrowed her gaze.

He glared.

Swede laughed. "It's all good. Let's go."

He grabbed Shadow's arm and tugged. Markus, his gaze knowing, led the way. Damn.

CHAPTER 7

ARIANNA WATCHED THEM leave. With Kevin's arms once again wrapped around her, she leaned against the closest tree for support and took the weight off her leg. She could have kept going, but she was damn glad she didn't have to. And that just made her a softie. Her father would roar at her to buck up and take it.

Like he had.

But she didn't even know if he was still alive. Right now she wanted to be back home safe and sound and preferably in her own bed where her leg could heal and she could forget this nightmare. She was so far from being in that position tears of exhaustion came to her eyes. It had to be the injury making her so weak. She wasn't normally like this.

"How bad is it, Ari?"

She managed to smile down at him. "Hurts like the dickens," she said with a smile. "Going to make walking difficult, but as far as being badly injured, don't worry. I'm not."

He appeared to be satisfied with that, then again he desperately wanted her to be fine so something in his world was okay. She could only hope they found their parents and they were still alive. For all her and her father hadn't seen eye to eye, she'd do a lot to hear him rage at her once again. He'd always been gruff and loud but it was who he was. She'd hoped for something closer but after her mother's death, Arianna had gone inside to deal with her loss and so had her father. They'd rarely met in any meaningful way after that. After Kevin was born she'd made a point of telling her father how he needed to change if he wanted his son to love and respect him and to have a relationship with him. He'd been angry like she couldn't remember ever seeing, but for a while he'd seemed to be there for Linda and the baby more.

But in the last few years he'd gotten busier, colder, and Kevin had gotten older. The relationship between the two had stretched very thin. That Linda hadn't much in the way of maternal hormones had further complicated manners. Then she was raising Kevin the way she'd been raised. As a showpiece to be seen and not heard. That might have worked for her decades ago, but Kevin needed so much more than that.

Arianna had started taking him for weekends where they'd done zoo trips and park outings, she'd taught him to swim and snowboard. She sucked at baseball, but they'd spent many a great hour playing catch. She knew her time with him was going to change once he grew into a teenager and needed his friends around more and more. He had friends now, but he still wanted to spend a lot of time with her.

Hard footsteps raced toward them.

Kevin lifted his head, his grip around her waist tightening.

Shit. She tried to lower herself to the ground so she was hidden by the brush a little more until she caught sight of who it was. Shadow. He raced toward her.

"Are they okay?" she asked anxiously.

"They are alive," Shadow said in a low voice. "But your father is in bad shape."

She knew that. But he was still alive and that meant he had a chance. Right? Shadow bent down and scooped her up, startling a gasp out of her. She wrapped her arms around him and held on. Glancing behind, she saw Swede walked silently carrying her father while Cooper carried her stepmother. Her father was unconscious, her stepmother had a large bruise on the side of her face and appeared to be in shock. The bruise probably meant she'd fought, hopefully to help her father. And for that she liked her stepmother for the first time in a long time.

Another man, nodded at her and disappeared into the bushes ahead.

"That's Mason," Shadow said in a low voice. "Hawk has gone ahead as well. Trying to clear a path for us."

"Why?" she asked. "There were two vehicles back there. Why couldn't we grab one of those?"

"Because we don't know if they have rigged them both," he answered in low tones, his gaze never stopping as they swiveled from one side to the other. "They also could have remote detonators. They could blow us up just when we thought we were safe."

"Right." She should have considered that. A sign of how she was really feeling. In fact, all she wanted to do was close her eyes and let this man carry her to safety. But then Kevin reached up and grabbed her hand. She squeezed his fingers. "I'm fine, Kevin. We've got Mom and Dad and we're heading to safety."

"Dad looks bad," he whispered just loud enough for her to hear. She stole a look behind her at her father's large but scrawny form in Swede's huge arms.

"I don't think Dad looks all that bad. It's just the giant carrying him that makes him look small and injured," she joked.

Kevin glanced back. "How come he's so big?"

"'Cause he ate his broccoli," she said with a laugh, knowing that was a sore point with her brother. He glared at her, then dropped his hand and slowed until he was beside Swede. She watched as he asked the big man something and grinned when Swede threw his head back and laughed. Then he nodded and said, "Absolutely."

"That was unfair," Shadow protested. "I don't like broccoli much either."

"Well, you're likely as big as you're going to get by now," she quipped. "And it's not just broccoli he won't eat, it's pretty much anything green."

"Oh. Well, I do like spinach and kale and chard."

"See, all the good stuff." Behind her Kevin chattered happily with Swede and Cooper, seemingly happy to run along beside everyone. "Thank you," she said.

"For what?"

She caught his sideways glance and beamed up at him. "For not treating him any different."

She was lifted in his arms as he raised and lowered his shoulders in a shrug. "He isn't any different. He's a young boy caught up in dealings that had nothing to do with him."

"True enough. Same for me."

"You have a special relationship with him."

The sentence was delivered as a statement and not a question, but she couldn't help but feel that there was a question in there anyway. "He's alone a lot. So I try to step in."

"Your parents travel?

"No," she said shortly. "They are busy."

"Right." And he fell silent.

She hadn't meant to shut the conversation down but what was she to do when the questions arose about how broken the relationship was between her brother and parents.

She sighed. "Linda is father's third wife. I'm a product of his second and my mother died of an overdose when I was little. I was raised by governesses until Father remarried. He chose another non–maternal type of woman, and I could see how Kevin was suffering. I'd moved out and he had a really hard time after that. So I stepped in to make his world a little happier when I could." She grinned as she glanced back to see him chattering nonstop behind her to the two men. "He's become remarkably normal in the meantime."

"You've done a good job raising him," Shadow said quietly.

"They raised him, I just helped to balance out the cold emptiness of living in that household. I remember it well."

"Your mother, was it deliberate?"

She didn't try to misunderstand. "I don't know. We'll never likely know. I was Kevin's age. And the cold front between my parents was already nasty. If she hadn't died, a divorce was in the immediate offing."

"Children are the real victims in a situation like that. It's not easy for anyone."

She studied his chiseled profile, detecting something long ago that had hurt him a lot. "Did your parents' divorce?"

"No." He gave her a smile completely devoid of any humor. "My father killed my mother instead."

SHIT, HE HADN'T meant to say that. In fact, he wasn't sure the last time he told anyone. It wasn't exactly ice breaker conversation.

And the last thing he needed was sympathy. If she showed him any pity, he'd dump her on the ground so she'd have to walk the rest of the way. Although he couldn't, it wasn't in him to do something like that. But...he held his breath and waited for her response.

When it came it blew him away.

"You know, I often wondered if that didn't cross my father's mind a time or two. I knew he didn't kill her as in he didn't force feed the pills down her throat, but I'm sure he was hoping she'd do it herself sooner than later." By the end of her sentence, she'd lowered her voice to a husky whisper as she glanced behind them to make sure her father couldn't hear her.

"What happened to his first wife?" he asked curiously. If that woman had died then maybe someone should be taking a look at the senator.

"Nothing so gruesome. They divorced and she has since remarried. I've met her at a couple of functions, but she's so similar to Linda that I'm wondering if he hasn't been searching for his first wife all over again. According to her, she's the one that left him."

Shadow nodded. "It happens."

"Yeah." She looked behind at Kevin, who given the circumstances, appeared to be in his element talking to Swede and Cooper. "Your friends are very nice."

Shadow stiffened.

"Kevin is really enjoying being around them," she said. "It's really good for him."

"What is?"

"Acceptance," she said simply. "If you saw his relationship to Dad and Linda, you'd see Kevin can't do anything right for my father who has such high expectations that *no one* can reach them and his mother who coddles him because she wants to protect him from such a big bad world. All because he's different."

"And you, did your father have the same high expectations for you?"

"Sure, but I was a disappointment from the outset so the expectations were lowered immediately."

He glanced at her. "In what way?"

"He only wanted a son."

Several hard clicks split the air.

Shadow froze, his arms tightening around her, his throat closing up as six men, assault rifles pointed their way, quickly surrounded them.

"Arianna," Kevin cried and ran toward her.

And a gun fired.

CHAPTER 8

ARIANNA CRIED OUT. But she couldn't see if anyone had been hit. Shadow had shoved her behind a tree and covered her with his big body. A volley of shots fired. Then more shots. Hidden behind the big man and worried about her family, she stayed pinned in place, shuddering. Her injury had changed something for her. Instead of being strong and capable she felt weak, in need of help. And hated that. Sure she did need the help, but she wasn't a victim. If she didn't get out of that mentality she'd become a liability. She didn't know where her brother was, nor the men who'd carried their parents. Surely they'd have been better off going back into the cabin. Especially given her father's condition.

She leaned her head back, eyes closed and waited. *Please stop the gunshots.* Her ears were ringing and she couldn't hear any voices over the loud noises. Surely everyone had to be dead by now. She shuddered.

Shadow twisted to look and his gruff voice, low and harsh, asked, "Are you okay? Are you hurt?"

"Hurt? No, just my leg." She stared at him fearfully. "Did they shoot Kevin?"

"They tried and missed." He shifted position so she could see around him. "He's with Swede."

And sure enough she could see her brother. He clung to Swede's back as the big man still carried her father. Jesus.

"Shouldn't we try to go back to the cabin?" she cried out, her heart hurting at the look of her father.

Shadow shook his head. "No. Reinforcements are coming. And an air ambulance will land on the lake in less than an hour."

She stared at him in hope. "Really?"

He nodded.

"Oh thank God."

"It's only been a few hours since you escaped the bedroom," he muttered. "It takes a little time to get some things done."

She wanted to laugh. Hell she really wanted to cry. Neither was an option. Their voices were so low she didn't think they'd carry, but they were taking a chance.

Thunder clapped overhead yet again. She jumped in surprise. Normally she loved storms, but if that heavy rain came back to soak them she'd be more than miserable and that was without taking her injured leg into account. An air ambulance sounded so normal and lovely she knew she was losing it. Several single shots sounded from across the way but not far enough away to make her happy. "You've got him pinned down," she whispered. "Finish him off."

"Can't until he shows himself."

"Then go get him," she said in a hoarse whisper. "I'm not going anywhere."

"Neither am I."

Of course he'd refuse to listen to reason. She leaned against the tree and closed her eyes. He could leave her and be back before she got to her feet. And she slowly slid down the damn trunk. It was dark, wet, cold and all she wanted to do was curl up in a ball and forget that his night had happened.

"Go," she ordered. "Then come back." She sensed his surprise, felt his doubt. She waved her hand to send him away. "I'm fine."

"Back in a moment," Shadow whispered, but before she understood what he meant, he was gone. She closed her eyes again. In this weather, no one was going to find her. It was too dark and ugly to bother looking.

Only she didn't have a moment to rest before he was there hauling her up onto her feet again. She shook off his help and stepped on her own. And shuddered. Damn it. She needed to be able to stand or he couldn't do what he needed to do. He gave her an arm for support. Yet again, she didn't protest. She kept walking and hung on. Stupid system. Why couldn't the good guys have nice vehicles to ride in? Instead they had no cabin and no wheels.

She was ready to round on him and tear a strip off him for not having the right equipment when a boom split the night sky. She cried out, instinctively crouching down as the night sky lit up all around them. Shadow slid an arm across her shoulders, tugging her up close. Then his voice, a harsh but reassuring whisper in her ear, said, "That's why we didn't go back to the cabin. If they were prepared to blow up the truck with your parents in it, likely they weren't going to leave much else behind either."

"My grandfather's cabin?" she asked, her voice cracking. She'd spent many happy weeks up here. But even thinking about those holidays it was hard to feel anything but shock at the moment as she watched the smoke curl in the sky.

It was gone.

"Could it have been the truck?" She barely got the words out when the second small boom sounded and she assumed that was the truck.

"They don't want us using their truck to escape either, I gather."

"No. They think we'll be handicapped by the terrain."

She looked around. "I have to admit it would be a lot easier to handle if my leg wasn't killing me."

"Not an issue. It's less than a mile to the lake, but we've been moving steady."

She shot him a look as if to say, *hell, no,* then realized that was really nothing of a distance and if they wanted to catch that plane…there wasn't much choice.

Except…as they slowly continued, the lack of light impeded their progress. How was the plane going to be able to land in this dark? When she asked Shadow, he said, "Dawn is only twenty minutes away. Bush pilot's don't live by the same rules that we live by."

"You? Rules? I don't think you follow any." She'd been trying to limp her way forward since starting again and now her leg was killing her, her breath coming out in harsh pants.

"Ready for some help?" he asked in a neutral voice, letting her know he'd noticed her struggle.

Shamefaced, she nodded. "Yes, please."

He swung her up in his arms and marched forward, his steps strong and sure in the dark.

She had to love that ability right now. Tired and sore and feeling very emotional for some reason, she gasped when she caught sight of the water twinkling through the trees.

"It's beautiful." Moonlight shone down on the ripples moving gently in the wind. She glanced back to see the progress the others had made. They were all close behind.

For all that he was tired and worn out, her brother was handling this adventure wonderfully. She was proud of him. "Kevin is doing really well."

"You both are."

She glanced at Shadow, her arms looped around his neck and shook her head. "No, we aren't. It's been a tough day for all my family."

He nodded but his scrutiny never strayed as he made his way to the water's edge. She loved that about him. Such focus. She could imagine he was the man to choose if you were alone on a desert island. He oozed competence. And that power that each of the SEALs exhibited was damn sexy.

But Shadow more so.

Knowing she shouldn't but unable to stop herself, she stroked his neck then leaned over and kissed his cheek again. She felt his start of surprise and had to wonder if he had much relationship experience. He always seemed so shocked at signs of affection. Every time she touched him, he seemed startled. As if not used to touch. Then again, this was a rescue mission, not a midnight tryst.

"What was that for?" he growled in low tones.

"Because I wanted to," she whispered. "Because it seemed like the right thing to do."

He gave her a slant-eyed look that said he didn't believe her. And just to be perverse, because she was being carried in a man's arms and probably not for much longer, and the experience was so new and different and, she admitted, quite surprisingly wonderful – she did it again. This time she kissed his jaw. Then dropped a kiss on his cheekbone. And one close to his ear.

A muscle in that beautiful chiseled jaw twitched.

And she realized something else. They'd been out long enough that he had a dark shadow growing along his neck and jawline adding to his dangerous look. It looked deadly good on him. How had she not noticed?

Shadow stopped and looked down at her. She smiled. "I know. You don't know what to do with someone like me. I'm different from other women. That's okay. Being different is allowed."

He shook his head. "And you talk too much." He slowly lowered her and pointed to the lake. Though she'd seen it peeking through the trees already, now the vista was open in front of her.

"It's beautiful. And I don't talk too much."

"Yes, you do." He smiled. "But maybe that's okay."

SHADOW SEARCHED THE rocky approach to the water. This was the most dangerous part of the rescue. With the new assault rifles the terrorists could shoot from hundreds of yards away allowing them to hide in the trees and pick off those standing on the beach – or worse, as they'd boarded the plane.

That they couldn't afford. They'd made it this far, now was not the time to lose focus. It could go perfectly or they could be slaughtered. Only one was acceptable. He studied the terrain. There were few places to hide on the beach. It wasn't sandy enough to burrow into, nor was it full of logs or large rocks to hide behind. Short and rocky, it was going to be hard to run across if that was their only choice. The trees were the enemies' best bet and that in itself was where he'd go. He needed to scout the line and see what the approach looked like from all angles.

He glanced at Arianna. She was pale but holding on. Good. The trip wasn't over yet. With a quick nudge of his head toward her, Shadow told Swede to watch her. Swede, still standing strong with the weight of the senator in his arms and the boy on his back, nodded.

Shadow, with a last look at the small group, disappeared into the woods. A hawk's call, long and lonely in the predawn light, told him Hawk was standing vigil on the captured soldiers. He'd barely heard what had happened but knew men were down. He just didn't know how bad. And the captives had another agenda. If they tried anything else, well they wouldn't be around for a third attempt. He quickly slipped through the trees.

The light was fascinating. Early morning, not quite night, not quite day. But getting lighter by the second. Hearing something up ahead, he slipped behind a large tree and waited. A huge buck stepped out onto the path. Shadow smiled. "It's okay, buddy, you go and get a drink."

The buck gave a light snort, his coat was damp from the night but steam rose off his back. He was on his morning trek to the lake for a drink. If he stayed to the one side he'd stay out of the path of the bullets. But if not...well Shadow would hate to see him get hurt.

The buck passed by, his gaze never straying from Shadow. After the big animal was gone, Shadow shifted his position to see if any unwanted attention had been attracted. But nothing moved. Uneasy but with nothing to show for it, he hunkered down and waited.

In the distance he could hear the hum of the plane as it approached. He tensed.

This was where it was going to get dicey. This was a Canadian military plane. It needed to be able to take the four family members out safely. No one could be left behind.

Swede gave a low cry. Shadow answered with the same series of raptor cries they'd perfected.

The plane's arrival had been noted.

He waited until the plane was visible. Still there was no movement. Either the enemy wasn't here or they had been in position already. They were terrorists, but that didn't mean they had outdoor training and maneuvers or were used to the sheer vastness of the Canadian wilderness. He'd spent months in the Yukon exploring a countryside that was so different than anything else he'd seen. If anyone needed to remember their connection to nature, spending a week in the woods up there would do it. Like here, there was so much country it was daunting. And stunning. And full of hardship, yet also offered great rewards.

The plane came in low and landed smoothly, just barely enough light to make it down. Thankfully, the storm had passed and the water was calm.

The first out of the plane were two soldiers with a stretcher.

Good, now to transport the casualties.

Swede met them at the edge of the water. Transferring the senator to the first stretcher and loading him on board took time. Knuckle baring time. According to Swede, the senator wasn't likely to make it. He hadn't regained consciousness once, and his old frail body had taken a beating that left Swede thinking major internal injuries. There'd been nothing they could do for him out there, but Swede hadn't wanted the old man who'd given his life to his country in a different way – to die alone. So he'd held the injured man to the end.

Now as the senator was loaded up into the small plane, Shadow could only wish him well. Then it was the wife's turn. He hadn't had a chance to ask Cooper about her, but Cooper would have said something if it had been bad. He smiled as Cooper got wet carrying Kevin to the plane. Kevin turned to check on his sister's progress.

Shadow had finally caught sight of something.

The enemy. Sneaking up on Arianna.

He lowered his rifle.

And took aim.

CHAPTER 9

A RIANNA WATCHED THE plane land with wonder. It had actually arrived. The night had begun to feel endless. With the moon fading back and the sky brightening as the sun rose but a long time away from sunrise, she studied the area in surprise. It felt locked in time. Frozen by the years. She didn't think anyone had been here since her last visit. Her favorite rocks and hollows leading to the lake where she'd spent hours of fun swimming were undisturbed. But it was not a world she wanted anything to do with right now.

"We're up next," Swede said. "Can you walk?"

"I can. But go ahead. Get Father on first." She hobbled forward, hating the pain biting into her with each step.

They walked together as a group until she realized how slow she really was. "Go and come back for me," she said.

Indecision rode him then he nodded abruptly and ran ahead. As in he picked up his feet and raced to the water's edge. The plane had coasted in as close as it could. She watched as two soldiers hopped into the water and carrying a stretcher, made their way over to Swede. Catching her breath and trying to hold back the waves of pain, she kept moving forward. Her brother was almost to the water now. He'd gone with Cooper. She took several more steps and gasped. Then a couple more. She didn't have far to go. And that plane was looking mighty fine. She watched her father being transferred and then it was her stepmother's turn. They were safe. *Thank God.* Cooper had picked up Kevin and carried him into the water to the men. He turned and called back, "Arianna?"

"I'm coming."

Swede started back toward her. She grimaced, but managed a smile for him.

And saw his expression change. He grabbed for his gun. She tried to hurry, but her leg gave out and she dropped to the ground.

Shots rained around her as rough hands picked her up and threw her over a shoulder and raced back toward the woods. "No," she screamed, flailing at the man who carried her. "Leave me alone."

More shots fired. This time toward the plane. As she struggled to free herself, the man shifted his grip on her leg and from a different direction grabbed at her wound. She screamed in agony.

The pain continued to ripple through her. She couldn't stop sobbing. Oh dear God. She swore he dug his fingers into the bullet hole on purpose.

"Shadow," she screamed, then couldn't speak as the pain kept rolling in deep greasy waves. So much damn pain. At least her family had made it. They'd been worse off than her. Tears rolled down her face as the plane started up and pulled away from the firestorm. Damn. She wanted to be on that plane. She so wanted to be leaving with the rest of her family. Instead, she was being carried deeper into the woods.

Shadow would save her. Surely.

Please.

A single bullet sounded. A man on the left dropped. She didn't even realize what had happened to him until he didn't get up again. Good. Bastards. Picking on her like that. Hanging down over the man's back, she could see he was dressed in khakis, so one of the damn terrorists. Of course. Through the pain she tried to focus. How many men were with her? Four. Well, three now. Any chance they were the last four? Because she was damn tired of this. The men were racing in a tight group and moving fast. Every step made her stomach roil in pain, and she came close to losing the peanut butter sandwich she'd eaten hours ago.

Then her eyes caught sight of something important. Could she?

She reached down and without letting herself second guess, she grabbed the man's handgun from the hip holster and pointed it at the head of the man running beside her.

Pop. Down he went. She turned to the next and clenched her fingers and shot him. The man carrying her squeezed her injury again and she screamed. And fired and fired and fired.

She couldn't stop even after the hammer fell and fell and no bullets came out.

"Easy. baby. Take it easy. They are all dead."

Shadow's voice washed over her. He'd come. He'd saved her again. Crying out, she opened her arms. He picked her up and cuddled her close.

She burst into tears.

"It's okay. I've got you." He rocked her gently in his arms as Swede and Cooper raced to their side. She couldn't stop crying. Her leg. Killing those men. Seeing the plane and knowing her family was gone. To know she'd been so close to flying out safely and having it all snatched away.

Finally, she wound down, and just lay against his chest. The odd sniffle still escaped but it was softer, faint. Then gulps of air as she tried to still the inside wretchedness.

Finally, she muttered, "Sorry."

He squeezed her gently. "Don't be. You needed that."

"Then how come I don't feel better?" But she did. She felt much better, but was that being safe again or being in Shadow's arms or from a complete breakdown in front of all the men? Then she remembered. She'd missed the flight. "They left without me, didn't they?"

"We sent them off. In a case like that, it's the best answer."

"I know." But she hated it. "I'm sorry I missed it."

"They couldn't wait. Your dad needs medical attention." Shadow hesitated. "He's in bad shape, Arianna."

She stared at him dry eyed. "He won't make it, will he?"

Shadow's lips curled down. She nodded. "I was afraid of that. He was always a stubborn old coot. But honorable."

"He's still alive, and we have to give him a chance so don't write him off just yet."

She nodded but inside she knew the chance was beyond slim. "Kevin and Linda?"

"Kevin is fine, although likely traumatized if he saw you carried off again. We're getting word to them…"

She winced. That would be hard on him. "The sooner the better."

"Right. And it looks like you're stuck with us," Swede said cheerfully.

"And what does that mean?" She tilted her head back to stare up at him and swiped her eyes. "Are we done here? Are there more assholes or did we finally get them all?"

Cooper coming up behind them laughed and said, "There are always more assholes."

"Any more around here?"

"Not likely. The man you took the picture of initially, have you seen him since?"

So much had happened she had to stop and think. Then frowned. "I'm not sure I did actually. He was here when we landed. That's when I snapped his picture. Then..." She shrugged. "I haven't seen him again."

Shadow nodded. "That would be my guess."

Leaning her head back against his chest, she thought about that man. "Are they going to come back after us again? After we get home?"

"You and your family? Not likely. Besides, they have pretty much decimated it already."

"Great," she said in sad tones. "I wasn't going to come, you know. I only came to spend time with Kevin and show him the great things to do here. The cabin was my grandfathers. My dad always used it as a getaway, but we haven't been here in years. I don't know what prompted it. Nor do I know why now. But out of the blue they made plans. I wasn't asked to join," she admitted, feeling the injury even now. "He wanted to bring Kevin, I think. Before the relationships with him and Kevin soured further."

"Was it bad?"

"Yes. I wonder if Father had been threatened before the trip." She frowned. "Maybe he figured getting away would save us."

"We'll figure it out. I know his house and office are being

turned upside down as we speak to find answers."

Right. Of course they were. And her place most likely.

"Can we leave now? Or are we waiting for the plane to come back and pick us up?"

"No, on the plane," Swede answered, "We have a truck back at camp. If you're okay to travel with us, we can take you back."

"Yes, please," she said in a small voice. She didn't have much choice but hoped it wouldn't take long. Her leg was killing her.

Still, she'd be with them, and Shadow. She'd take an extra hour with him. She struggled to try and get to her feet, with Shadow helping her to stand. Waves of pain rolled through her. She focused on her breathing, trying hard to keep it together. She hadn't even put her bad leg down.

When she could, she lowered her foot to the ground and gently put her weight on it. And whimpered. Swaying in place and still holding onto Shadow – or rather Shadow holding onto her, she lowered her head and sucked in deep breaths. She could do this. She had to do this. Why wasn't she on that damn plane?

Just when she was ready to break down and ask for help, she was swung up into Shadow's arms and told, "Now lie quiet."

She wondered at the lie quiet comment. Was that because of the enemy or because he was tired. Or to stop her from fighting the help. Damn she didn't know anymore. But he couldn't carry her all the way back. That was too far. "I'm too heavy for you to carry for so long," she protested.

He slanted a look her way and stayed quiet.

"Maybe you could take turns and that would ease the load for you," she suggested.

The only response was to squeeze her tighter.

She subsided. Fine. Let him suffer. She planned to enjoy the experience. Or would have if it didn't hurt so damn much. She closed her eyes and realized she'd tensed to the point of resisting him. And that she didn't want. She needed to relax. But given her leg and her fear that he'd shuffle her and hurt her more... Then she understood how he'd lifted her into his arms. With her injured leg crossed over her healthy one. So as to not hurt it more. And he couldn't grab it accidentally this way either.

As in he'd done everything he could to keep her safe and out of harm.

She sighed and relaxed against him yet again. "Thanks," she muttered.

"You're welcome."

She smiled and closed her eyes.

Damn, he was fine.

DAMN, SHE WAS fine.

And he was an idiot. But he kept remembering his panic when he'd seen her spirited away in the group of terrorists. They'd swooped down onto the beach sending out a hail of fire covering their movements and snatched her up. His heart had damn near stopped, but his feet were already on the move.

He'd raced into the trees following the beach to get her before they could take her out of the area and be lost forever. He'd seen too many people disappear in this life. And that wasn't something he was willing to let happen to Arianna. She was his. No, she wasn't his, but she was his. He rescued her once, or was it twice by now? Maybe three times. Who was counting?

He didn't dare lose her to these assholes. Who knew what they'd do to her now they'd lost the rest of the family. He remembered the look on her face when she saw the plane taking off in the opposite direction. To know she'd been left behind. It would haunt him forever. Then screaming in pain, her body twisted in agony as her leg was gripped to keep her under control. Did she give in? Hell, no. She managed to get that gun and kill three men all on her own. It was at the end when she just kept shooting he'd felt his heart break. She'd been doing her damnedest to maintain some control and then lost it.

He was so proud of her.

Now she lay curled up lightly sleeping in his arms. Like hell he was going to hand her off to the others.

Swede walked up beside him. "Do you want me to carry her for a spell?"

Sensing the humor in his voice and seeing the grin on his friend's face, Shadow shot him a look. "No. I'm fine," he said calmly.

"Better than fine from the way I see it," Cooper said cheerfully. "Look at that. The one man I didn't think would ever fall – has not only fallen but done an all-out tumble in front of us."

Shadow refused to answer.

Arianna shifted uneasily in his arms as if disturbed by the men's voices. Shadow glared at his friends for waking her.

Swede smirked and stepped in front to lead the way. Cooper, a huge grin covering his face fell in behind to bring up the rear. Their radio whispered in his ear. Mason and Dane were still at the camp looking for an update. Only half listening Shadow keep watch on the surrounding woods as Swede reported that the plane had left with the senator, wife and son. That Arianna was injured and had been taken again. That she was back with them and four more of the enemy were dead.

There was going to be a hell of a cleanup done here. The bodies all had to be collected and dealt with. He hoped the Canadians would handle that part. Mop up was a bitch. He needed IDs of the dead men, but that was the only thing he wanted from these men now.

They had just under a mile to go. Without breaking stride and on guard they trekked through the woods toward the rest of their team. As they came to a half mile out, Hawk joined them, his sharp look going from one face to the other then dropping to Arianna's wan features in Shadow's arm. "How badly is she hurt?"

"Gunshot through the thigh."

Hawk asked, "Not bleeding out?"

"No. It's stopped or had stopped until the bastards grabbed her."

Hawk didn't waste any time. He led the way into camp, letting the others know they were approaching. At the edge, Shadow stopped and stared, using the time to study what was going on ahead of him. He had no intention of entering if she wasn't safe here.

Mason walked over. Shadow clarified, "Gunshot to the thigh, missed the bone."

"Good. She's asleep?"

"Yeah, the last attack finished her."

"Tell me?"

Still standing, Shadow quickly explained what happened. Hawk and Dane joined them.

Hawk stared down at the woman in Shadow's arms. "She killed them?" he asked incredulously. "All of them?"

Shadow nodded.

Dane whistled. "She's a keeper."

Shadow glared at him. Hawk slapped him on the shoulder. "Let's lie her down on the back of the truck. We need to check out that leg. See if the bastards made it any worse."

That made sense, but it was damn hard trying to let her go. It took three tries with his friends watching before he could finally lower her down to the back of the truck and step back.

Finally he managed it.

Swede, a hand on his shoulder said, "It's tough, isn't it?"

"What is?" he asked, frowning down at the woman who had somehow gotten under his skin.

"Finding what you want and knowing it's yours but also knowing you don't have the right to keep her."

He lifted his head to stare at his friend and finally understood what he meant.

Damn.

Swede was right.

It sucked.

CHAPTER 10

W AKING TO PAIN sucked. Waking to horrific pain, sobbing, and with tears rolling down her eyes, yeah that topped her list of shitty mornings. Arianna tried to roll over to get away from the fire in her leg and couldn't. Not only couldn't she get away from the pain it seemed she couldn't move at all. And someone was blubbering over and over again. She couldn't think for the noise. She shuddered at the onslaught mental, auditory, and physical.

"Arianna, take it easy. We're working on your leg. You've just woken up. You're okay."

It was that last sentence that got her.

"I'm not okay," she snapped, bolting upright only to get instantly forced back down by Swede and Shadow. As she stared up at them, her breathing raw, she slowly realized where she was and why.

And that she was the one blubbering.

How humiliating. By this time she wanted to really bawl. Rail at the unfair world that saw her still in the wilderness being treated to field kit type medical treatment. Like really, wasn't she supposed to wake up in a hospital somewhere with nice white sheets and shitty food? Not staring at these two bad-asses who were holding her down.

Tears filled her eyes. Then someone lit her injury on fire and she screamed. Then whimpered as the waves of darkness pushed her back under. She could see oblivion. Escape was there – just out of her reach.

She reached for it – and fell under its spell again.

When she woke the second time it was to the cold. Shivers slid up and down her long frame like fingers on guitar strings. How had it become so chilly outside? It was summer, right?

And the sun shone overhead, didn't it? As she lay there shivering she couldn't help but think her world had completely spun out of control. She was so tired. And there were men all around her. She could hear the strange voices outside and could see some of them. Did they know she was here? She studied the face of the man closest to her, but she didn't recognize him. Her glance slid over to the two men talking together beside him, and she didn't know them either. Her panicked mind didn't know if that was a good thing or bad. Shaking so badly she could barely move, she huddled back against the side of the truck.

A man's voice reached her. "She's waking up. Where's Shadow? Swede? Even Cooper."

The man who'd been sitting closest to her reached out and gently grabbed her hand.

She snatched it back. She knew this man was dressed the same as the good guys, but her mind couldn't make heads or tails of any of this. Inside she couldn't seem to think or do anything rational. All she wanted to do was get up and run, but everything below her waist hurt like shit.

"Arianna, take it easy." In the background she heard someone say, "Get one of the other SEALs."

She partially recognized the voice, but she didn't know the

man. She'd heard that voice last night, right? But then she'd been snatched up by a lot of men last night too. And been hurt by them.

Was this the man who'd hurt her?

She swallowed hard and stared at him saucer-eyed.

"No one is going to hurt you. Your leg is injured. We had to clean and bind the wound." He spoke slowly and carefully, his hand gently stroking her arm. "No one here is going to hurt you."

She shuddered. "Where are the others?"

He smiled at her. "They are coming. You'll see them in a few minutes. I'm Dane. You heard my name mentioned before, surely," he said in a teasing voice. "I know you did."

Another face slid into view behind Dane. She narrowed her gaze at him but didn't recognize him either.

"No need to worry. I'm Mason. Hawk is here too. The three of us were keeping a watch on the far side of where you were and holding the prisoners back," he said cheerfully. "Not a very glorious job this time but there was lots of communication. You're looking for one of the other three goofs. They went back to make sure there were no injured men after the bombs went off."

Prisoners? Communications? Bomb?

At the word bomb her eyes widened. "They blew up my grandfather's cabin?"

"They did. And their own truck apparently. Not sure about the other rig. We could use it right now."

Rig? Right, the terrorists had brought another vehicle.

Slowly the distorted memories filtered into her brain and arranged to a more or less recognizable pattern. She relaxed back slightly. She studied the truck bed she lay in. There was something beneath her, but it wasn't soft or comfortable. And she was so damn cold. Just when she thought it was getting better, a wave washed over her making her teeth chatter.

"So cold," she whispered.

"I can help with that," Mason said before he disappeared from view.

Like that was a help. But he returned a few minutes later with a big heavy coat that he laid over the front of her. "Now just rest. We'll be leaving here soon."

"Leaving?"

"Yes, we're driving you to a small town close by and will make arrangements to get you home from there."

"Oh." She didn't even know what to say to that. Drive to a town didn't sound great considering how she was feeling right now. A small town wasn't going to have a doctor or even a medical clinic. And arrangements to get home, although home sounded lovely that whole arrangement thing sucked.

But home was the nirvana she was looking for right now.

She snuggled under the heavy coat, loving the familiar smell to it, and closed her eyes.

"How is she?"

Shadow walked into the camp and straight to the truck. He nodded to Evan who stood at the edge. Markus, who'd followed him back, veered off to talk to Evan. Always alert, always on guard.

Good thing. Too bad he didn't have good news to report. They hadn't been able to salvage either of the other two vehicles – or anything of what remained of the cabin. In fact, it was a hell of a mess. He hated to see it. The cabin had been prime in its day. Now it resembled charred toothpicks.

"She's awake. Cold, hurting and worried."

"Worried about what?" Shadow frowned at Dane.

"You, you weren't there when she woke up."

"And?" Shadow studied the men around him suspiciously. He was often the butt of the jokes in the group but no more than anyone else. Only when the others were grinning at him like he could see them doing now, well, that was guaranteed to set off his radar.

"She woke alone, she was scared," Mason said in a calm low voice. "And she was worried. About where she was and more so about where you were."

Shadow turned to look at his friend. "Worried about me?" He raised an eyebrow at the thought. In the physical surroundings he was the last person here she needed to be worried about. "She's just not feeling well."

"Ah, it's more than that," Cooper said at his side. "She's sweet on you."

Shadow shook his head. "Hell no she isn't. I rescued her, she's grateful, that's all." And he sure didn't want gratitude from her. Nor did he want her to mistake gratitude as being something more. It wasn't.

"Go and see her," Mason said. "Regardless of what's going on, her mental state is going to have a huge impact on her healing. She needs to know you're okay. So set her mind at ease."

With the others grinning, Shadow walked to the big rig and pulled the heavy canvas back. "Ari," he said, his voice soft, gentle. Damn men. Making him think in one direction as hope blossomed inside. But it wasn't to be. He knew that. He just had to remember.

"Shadow?" she asked sleepily from under the heavy coat. He stared at the coat. It was his. Trust the guys yet again.

"Yeah, it's me."

She sat up, and he couldn't help but stare. Tear stained cheeks, red puffy eyes, but their vision was clear, direct and warm. Hell. She opened her arms. When he didn't reach for her, her lower lip trembled. Making him feel like an ass. Too damn bad if the men were watching. He opened his arms and with a small cry she fell into them.

"I was so scared when I woke up," she confessed against his neck, snuggling close. "I didn't recognize anyone."

"We had to go back and check out the condition of the cabin." And retrieve the bodies of the terrorists. They were stacked off to the side under tarps. There were only two vehicles here. Another was on its way. He moved so he could sit on the tailgate and hold her.

"Is it okay?" she sniffled.

"Well, it's gone if that's what you mean," he said quietly. "I'm sorry for that."

She smiled up at him. "Thanks. But I have the memories and that's what is important."

Pulling back slightly, she asked in a low voice, "Is there any update on my family? Is my father okay?"

He shook his head, hating to not be able to give her the news she needed to hear. "We don't know anything yet. Communication up here is spotty at best."

Her face fell, yet she nodded in understanding. He felt like he'd failed.

"It's okay. I know he's in good hands, and everyone is doing what they can for him. For all of us," she said gently.

He sighed. "That attitude will get you walked all over in this world."

"And sometimes it brings good things. I know there are a lot of growly bear people out there, scammers, and just really bad nastiness, but that doesn't mean there isn't room for people like me."

"And what are the people like you."

She smiled and snuggled close. "People who believe in heroes and unicorns, rainbows and chocolate chip ice cream at midnight." She yawned at the end, and he wasn't sure he'd heard her correctly. But when he went to ask what any of those things had in common and to ask if she understood unicorns didn't exist, he heard deep peaceful breathing and tiny delicate snores.

Damn.

He glanced out at the camp the men were tearing down. He should be helping them. But as he glanced down at the angel in his arms, he didn't want to leave her. In a voice just barely audible, he said, "I've never seen unicorns and haven't met any heroes, but maybe they are possible because until last night, I'd never met a real live angel, either."

And he dropped a gentle kiss on her forehead.

CHAPTER 11

W HEN SHE WOKE the next time, the pain had dulled to a deep agonizing throb but was no longer the hot searing rage in her leg. But she was alone. And that she was getting to hate.

She'd spent too much of her lifetime alone. In spite of her upbringing, she'd somehow managed to create that Pollyanna attitude that she'd have a good day if she could just believe in it hard enough. And for the most part she was content with her life. It wasn't awe shattering or full of excitement, but there was something comforting to it. And now she realized the comforting part was the familiar part. She was alone. Somehow that had become the norm, and one she had become satisfied with. She'd been happy in the few relationships she'd had until the men had wanted to move in. That hadn't been for her. At the time she'd just figured she hadn't been ready for the commitment.

And she hadn't been. In that she hadn't been ready to give up that comfort of what she knew – had known all her life – a solitary lifestyle.

What would it take for her to give that up?

The right man, of course. Because in that way she'd not be giving up anything, she'd be gaining.

Up until then though it seemed like she'd be losing.

So they weren't the right men.

Shadow stole into her mind. Was he the right man?

Not possible. Look at the differences in their worlds. He wouldn't want someone like her. He lived in the shadows. She lived in the sunlight. She could take a walk in the shadows but only a short one. She couldn't live there. She'd have to take the rays of sunshine from her world to warm up the darkness in his.

In his? What was she thinking? He wasn't for her.

But he could be.

No. He couldn't be.

Yes. She wiggled with delight. She knew she was living a fantasy in her mind at the thought, but if there was ever anyone who needed her to bring light into his world, it was Shadow.

When his face appeared in front of her she figured she must be dreaming. She beamed at him. "Good morning."

His response was slow to come. "Good morning, how are you feeling?"

"If I don't move, fine. Thank you for asking."

He rolled his eyes, making her grin and prompting her to ask, "How are you feeling?"

"I'm fine," he said. "I'm not the one injured."

"No," she said cheerfully, reaching out a hand to cup the side of his face. "But you are the one who's feeling guilty."

And damn if a dark stain didn't wash up his neck.

Oh no. "You shouldn't feel that way, you know that, right?"

"I left you alone," he said curtly. "There is no other way to feel."

"You had more things to do than babysit me. You're a hot shot sexy SEAL and babysitting is not a required course."

Again that glance slanted her way.

"Sexy?"

She flushed. She had said that, hadn't she? Ah well. "It's the truth," she admitted. "I'd say all of you are, but then you'll discount that you aren't and of course you're the sexiest man here."

Surprised and obviously discomforted, he said, "Do you always worry about other people's feelings like that? It's got to be wearing."

"It can be, but I am who I am. Sunshine and roses, remember?"

"Yeah, and what happens when you end up in moonlight instead," he asked curiously.

And because there was nothing mocking in his tone, she answered, "I usually get depressed until I can cheer myself up."

"And how'd you do that?"

She realized he was serious. "By listening to music, spending time with friends or Kevin, singing and dancing..." She shrugged. "There are lots of ways."

He glanced behind them at the work going on.

"What do you do when you get down?" she asked.

Startled, he answered willingly enough. "I tell myself to get over it and get back to work."

Someone called his name. And he left. Just like that.

She lay back down and realized they needed to get moving. And the sooner the better. She had no idea how long she'd been out, but as she peeked through the back the sun was still rising. Good. They hadn't been waiting on her. She shifted experimentally, wondering how mobile she was going to be as she desperately needed a bathroom. And of course there was no such thing available. She had no qualms about a walk to a secluded part of the bush except for that *walk* part.

Crouching down was going to be damn near impossible. And she needed to go. As she shuffled her butt to the edge of the truck, she realized she no longer wore her jeans. In dismay she stared down at the oversized sweatpants. Donated by someone on the team most likely. But on her, yeah they were huge. Thankfully whoever had changed her left her panties on. And the leg did move easier in warm loose sweats. But she must look a fool.

She laughed. Oh well, better a warm fool than a cold one.

She lowered her legs over the edge of the tailgate and sat up. The place was full of activity. There were men sitting in another vehicle all handcuffed together. And dressed in khakis. She studied their blank faces, surprised to see any still alive.

The rest of the men appeared to be leaning over the hood of a truck poring over something. A map most likely. She carefully turned and crept down the back of the truck and hobbled to the front. There out of sight, and using the front grill to hold onto, she managed to lower herself on one leg. She quickly went to the bathroom. As she struggled back to the rear of the truck, Shadow stepped into her path.

"You know you could have asked for help."

She looked at him wryly. "Yeah, to what, wipe my butt?" She grinned.

He smirked. "If need be then yes."

She shuddered, and quickly said, "No thanks. I was fine."

"You were going to make sure of it, even if you weren't, right?"

A bit convoluted but she did finally get it. "Hey, if I can save myself that bit of humiliation, I'm all for it. You'd do the same."

"I would," he said immediately. "But if I couldn't…"

"Right. If I get that bad, I'll let you know." *Not*, she added mentally. It would be hard to be in that position. She understood that everyone might need such assistance at one point in time but she'd hope that was at least eighty years away.

And she gave thanks to the world around her that she was in as good a shape as she was. With his help, she got back up on the tailgate so she could sit and watch.

HE'D WATCHED HER struggle to get down off the truck, her furtive glances to see if anyone was watching. He'd soon realized she'd needed a bathroom break. Something that was much easier in the woods for him than her – especially given her injured leg. He'd waited, trying to give her space and independence and had to grin when she'd returned slowly, painfully, but in one piece.

"Go. You're useless here anyway," Mason said in a hard tone but his eyes were twinkling.

Shadow gave him a flat look. But when he spun around to check on her the next time, Swede gave him a push in her direction.

"It's your turn. Go be a hero."

And he'd left. Now that she was safe again and he'd rejoined the men, it was as if he had an inner sense when she moved or needed something. Like what was with that?

"We're leaving in twenty minutes. We'll head to a town and see if we can get her a faster return trip," Mason said. "Her leg is healing, but I can't be sure there isn't muscle damage inside that she'd need a doctor to fix. And the sooner for that the better."

Shadow nodded. "Which rig? I'll get her settled in." He glanced around. "She had a pack at one time too."

Cooper nodded to the side. "It's over there."

Shadow caught sight of the red canvas pack. He waited to hear the end of the conversation then walked over and grabbed the bag. Returning to her side, he watched her face brighten. And inside he sighed. He had it bad. Anything to see her smile. Particularly when it was directed at him.

"Thank you," she cried. "I wondered if I'd see it again."

He laid it down beside her.

She opened it immediately and rummaged through. "I have spare jeans in here."

"Not jeans. Too hard to get on and off for cleaning the leg wound."

She frowned and plucked at the material on her legs now. "But these belong to someone. I have to give them back."

"They are mine and I don't need them right now."

With a gasp, she threw her arms around him and hugged him. Damn. He couldn't help wrapping his arms around her and holding her tight. For a moment, he glimpsed the sunlight as it broke through the shadows. Then she dropped her arms and the light disappeared.

But it was enough. He stared at her in wonder. Is that what it was like to not be alone? He couldn't ask her. Knew it wasn't the time for such a question and she likely wouldn't know as she lived in the sunlight and had no idea the world was cloaked in shadows like he did.

As he watched she went back to rummaging through her bag. She pulled out a chocolate bar in triumph. Then she stared at its size before shoving it back inside.

"You aren't hungry?"

"I'm starved," she confessed. "But everyone is, and I can't break a bar that small to give everyone a piece."

What? He studied her again. "You don't have to share with everyone."

"Have to, no I don't. But I want to. So it will have to wait until later when there are less people around so everyone can have a taste."

Not understanding her logic, he said, "We're leaving in the other truck." He watched as Swede started loading the back of their rig. "I need to get you over there now."

"Is it big enough," she asked in a low voice, mentally counting the men in the area. "Maybe I should wait here until later."

"For what later?" he asked. "This is your ride. Now or never."

She nodded. "Now then. If you have room for me."

He sighed and swooped down and caught her up in his arms, startling a squeak out of her as he carried her and her backpack to the truck beside them. Swede seeing them coming, opened up the back passenger door. "Your ride, princess."

She beamed at him. "Thanks, I appreciate it."

"Well, it's not a plane but we'll get you home one way or another."

Shadow helped her sit on the bench then watched as she scooted back so her leg was resting on the seat. She took up most of the back. That wouldn't last long. "Rest. We'll be leaving in just a few minutes."

She leaned forward. "But there's not enough room for everyone."

"There will be," he whispered back.

That she'd be riding on his lap was something he understood, but she had yet to figure out. He was looking forward to seeing her reaction when she finally did.

CHAPTER 12

S HE GAVE HIM a flat stare when she finally understood that his picking her up and settling her on his lap wasn't temporary. As in this was the way she'd be riding to the next town.

He grinned at her. She glared at him.

Swede, sitting in the front, chuckled. She wanted to smack him. Beside Shadow sat Cooper and then Hawk. Mason drove and Dane had been pinched into the middle in the front. Markus and Evan had stayed behind to help the Canadians out.

She turned her head toward Shadow. "I told you I wouldn't fit."

"And I told you, you would."

She sighed. "You're being difficult," she announced.

"No, you are."

"You can't always tell me I'm wrong." She gave him a curt nod for punctuation.

"If you are, I can," he countered.

She gasped. "Are you saying I'm always wrong? That's mean," she cried.

Shadow rolled his eyes and stared out the window.

She caught sight of Hawk's smirk. "He's being mean, isn't he?"

Immediately Hawk agreed.

Right. He knew what his role was. "You should tell him," she said with a nod.

"Shadow, you're being mean," Hawk instantly said.

A low rumble of laughter rippled through the truck.

She crossed her arms. "It's easy to see which of you have partners," she snapped.

Cooper eyed her curiously. "How's that?"

"All those men know better than to argue," she replied, glaring at Shadow. "Then there are those who haven't learned that lesson yet."

And this time the men cracked up.

Cooper immediately started whistling a tune she vaguely recognized. "What's that song?" she asked.

Straight–faced he opened his mouth to answer, but Shadow's arm straightened and belted him across the chest.

Cooper coughed several times.

Arianna rounded on Shadow. "What was that for?" she cried. "We were just having a nice conversation."

He glared at her. But never said a word.

"See, you're just being mean again."

The men in the truck were all trying to suppress chuckles. Cooper the most of all. She studied him suspiciously. "He didn't hurt you, did he?"

"Just my feelings," Cooper managed in a deadpan tone of voice.

"Oh, I'm so sorry. Shadow is like that," she explained to the captive audience. "He rarely explains himself. He probably just didn't want you to give the wrong answer and be embarrassed." She rounded on Shadow who was staring at her in apparent fascination. "If you'd explain yourself a little more it would be easier on everyone. Use those words I know you have inside," she said nicely. "It really will get easier over time."

"You talk too much," he snapped.

Her lower lip trembled.

An odd silence sounded in the truck.

Cooper nudged Shadow. "Fix it."

"It's okay," she said in a low voice. "It's not the first time he's told me that."

And she was jerked forward and kissed hard.

Eagerly she threw her arms around him and kissed him back only he suddenly pushed her back and jammed her up against his chest.

Happily she snuggled in close. "I'm sorry for calling you mean. You're really a pussycat inside."

SHADOW SIGHED. WHAT the hell was he going to do with her? Calling him a pussycat. Hell, he was a fucking panther in the dark.

"Isn't that nice," Hawk murmured from the other side. "I'm happy we have a pussycat in the truck."

The group sniggered.

Mason, who was driving, came to Shadow's rescue. "But as I recall we've all had similar scenarios happen to us."

"So damn glad that's over," Dane said with feeling. "What a confounding stage of life that was."

Confounding. Yeah, that was the word for it. Shadow stared down at the woman snuggled up against his chest. How could she be such a powder puff right now and yet be the same woman who'd signaled for help in the cabin window and crawled from tree to tree to knock an attacker down because he was hunting her brother? And that was without mentioning the three men she shot to death.

Now she was curled up like a baby as innocent as could be.

Yeah, he was confounded. Not only by her behavior but her thought processes. She seemed to think he was... Hell, he didn't know what she thought. He'd say wonderful but that was ridiculous. Yet by body language alone, he had to consider it. She didn't go to any of the other men on her own.

"Next time," Cooper announced, "there's a beautiful woman who needs rescuing, I get the job."

Several of the guys chuckled. But everyone in the truck knew what he meant.

Shadow wondered if fate played a hand in picking the rescuers. Then again, he'd rescued dozens of people and outside of normal gratitude they never seemed to show any interest in him. Yet every time lately they'd been on a mission and a woman had been in trouble, she'd hooked up with one of his teammates. And he might have had a hand in that last time too. He'd known Swede had been sweet on Eva for years. But she was – in his head – forbidden. Shadow had even helped send him to her rescue, hoping it would be enough to change things for his friend. And it had.

More than anyone had expected.

That wasn't the same thing right now. He'd never met Arianna before.

And there'd been more than just him involved in this rescue, but Arianna had apparently picked him. Shadow just didn't know to what extent she was favoring him.

But he wanted to.

He leaned back and closed his eyes. It was going to be a long trip. All the more so the way she slumbered. His body was more than aware of the feminine body on his lap. It didn't need any more incentive to wake up and pay attention.

Arianna shuffled slightly and moaned.

He groaned as her rounded bottom slid across his groin.

It was going to be one fucking long trip.

CHAPTER 13

S HE DOZED, SHIFTED to get comfortable, surfaced then dozed again.

When she finally woke it was to see a different terrain outside the truck window. She sat up and heard Shadow's gasp, then groan.

"Oh, I'm sorry," she cried out in a hushed whisper as she tried to wiggle into a better position.

He grabbed her hips and stopped her movements.

"Is that better?"

"Yes," he said between gritted teeth. Then he took a deep breath. "Just stop your damn wiggling."

She glared at him. "Are we back to that? Remember I said there was no room in here for me."

"Are we back to that," he said perversely enjoying getting her riled up again. "I said there *was* enough room for you."

She sighed and collapsed down again. "You're getting into your mean mode again."

He hugged her close. "No, I'm not."

She was quiet for a long time. "Where are we? I thought we'd have reached the next town by now."

"Shouldn't be much longer. Although there is some concern that there isn't much there. Apparently, small Canadian towns in the north are often only a collection of houses and not much else."

"I remember that from last time. Nowhere close enough to drive to. It's like six hours to the main center."

"Right. If need be, we can do that."

She sighed. "I hope we don't have to. I'm getting awfully hungry."

"You've still got your chocolate bar," he reminded her. As she perked up and looked around for her bag, he added, "Don't bother. It's in the back with the rest of the gear."

He reached for her hips to stop her from moving too much, but she didn't notice. Her sore leg was stretched across Cooper's legs, giving him no room to go anywhere. Poor Cooper.

Shadow reached into his pocket and pulled out her bar. "Here. I pulled it out earlier."

With a beaming smile she took it, opened it, and carefully broke it into seven pieces.

He watched her as she handed out a piece to everyone. One piece was slightly larger than the others and one was slightly smaller. The small one she kept for herself, and she gave him the biggest piece.

Of course she did. He was looking after her so well. She wished she could give him more.

But there wasn't anything else to give him. At least not here.

She studied the small town as they drove past. There were a few houses dotting the highway from miles out. Normal in a way. If you were a loner and preferred wilderness to city, like these people did, they all wanted to live on the edge of town. No matter how small the town was. And as small towns went she'd have said this was the smallest she'd seen. Barely a community and not big enough to be considered a township.

There was a small store in the center and before they knew it they'd passed it. Mason slowed and pulled off on the side of the highway. "Did anyone see a store or medical center or...anything? What's the chance we haven't hit the main town yet?"

"I saw a store," Arianna said, twisting to look behind them. "But nothing else."

Several others confirmed the store.

Mason had the truck turned around and pulled up to the store, which appeared to double as a gas station, except from the ancient pumps in the back, she wasn't sure she trusted anything that came out of these machines.

But a bathroom would be good.

The door opened behind her, and Shadow exited with her in his arms, somehow making the movement natural and graceful.

"Any chance of a bathroom?" she whispered, studying the gas station.

"Likely inside." He held her steady as she regained her footing and hobbled around a few steps to keep the blood circulating.

The air had a freshness to it she loved. She took a deep breath. She hadn't had a chance to notice the air this morning with everything going on but now on the way home...she sniffed happily. "Smells nice."

"Not in here it doesn't." Mason stepped back out of the store.

She turned slightly to see him. The grim visage had her heart and stomach plummeting. "What's wrong?"

"The store owner is dead." Mason nodded to the interior behind him. "Been dead at least a day."

"Shit," she heard Shadow mutter. He dropped her arm that she'd been using for support and said, "I have to go look."

Arianna watched mutely as Shadow disappeared into the store. Swede, being the guy he was, had stepped into Shadow's place, but he'd opened the back of the truck first and was now armed. She took a deep breath and let it out carefully.

"I'd hoped this was all over," she said in low tones.

"It was," Swede said. "Until we found another dead man."

"Do you think he was killed by the kidnappers?"

"Likely, but we need to find out for sure. Can't guess on this one. And that means talk to anyone here who is left to talk to us."

She gasped and turned to him. "You don't think they are all dead."

"No. I don't." He immediately shook his head. "But the storekeeper was killed yesterday, that's enough time for others to go into hiding."

Yet his voice didn't match his words. He stared behind the vehicle and studied the houses across the road. One small house on the corner in particular. And the fluttering curtains in the window. "Think they are in there?"

"Oh yeah, the question is who and are they wary naturally or did they see something that has terrified them," he muttered, shifting to study the other buildings.

She looked around. There were a dozen homes all centered near the store but not a sign of anyone. As her gaze swept past the store, the door opened and Dane and Cooper... Shadow walked out. The dark overcast and chiseled faces said so much. She wanted to hobble closer, reach out and let him know she was here, but the look on his face said he wouldn't likely recognize the support if she did. It made her sad. She watched him disappear around the corner of the building. That reminded her she needed a bathroom. She looked for a restroom sign but didn't see one.

"What are you looking for?" Swede asked, an intent look in his eyes.

She scrunched up her face. "A bathroom."

"I'll look." He motioned toward Cooper who walked closer. Then Swede took off around the building. She smiled at Cooper. "Hey."

He grinned. "Hey back. How's the leg?"

"Fine." Then she shrugged, admitting with a wry grin, "As long as I don't try to use it."

He chuckled. "You're coming due for more pain killers if you feel the need."

She frowned, considering. "I'm not too bad at the moment"

"Good, then we'll leave it for a little bit longer. What we don't want is to leave it so long that you end up suffering until the new meds kick in."

Yeah, that didn't sound like fun.

But the pain killers knocked her out and made her thinking fuzzy, forcing others to carry her sorry ass around until she was awake again. "Maybe when we get this mess settled…" She motioned to the town around them.

"*This* has nothing to do with you. If we can't determine that you're safe here then you're not staying. We'll figure out another way to get you home."

"Are you guys going home?" she asked cautiously. "Maybe I could go with you?"

"Maybe," he said cheerfully. "I'm all for it. Then at least we know you're safe. But you need medical attention now, not in a few days when we get there."

"Seems like we're always against the clock." She hoped the damage to her leg was minor but had no way to know. Cooper's good drugs kept her from having to worry about it too much. But she wanted to have the full function of it.

"So we need a hospital to check you over and then we can make plans."

Sounded good. But she suspected she'd soon be parted from these men. That was sad. She was so proud to have known them. They were heroes. And they'd done right by her. If they needed her to buck up and be left behind so they could carry on tracking her kidnappers then so be it.

Swede arrived. "Found it. It's at the back."

He didn't give her an opportunity to protest but swooped her up into his arms and carried her laughingly protesting around to the back of the building.

The door was open. He set her down inside then stepped out and closed the door. She wanted to laugh at the look on his face. He'd been dying to ask if she wanted help but knew she wouldn't take it kindly. He was a good man. Just like the rest of them.

Privacy and a real toilet, and look, running water. She smiled with joy. Oh the simple things in life. She quickly used the toilet then set about to wash the rest of her...at least what she could reach. The paper towels were scratchy on her neck and face but the warm water was a delight. When she finished she opened the door and hobbled out.

Into Shadow.

"Oh," she stumbled back and cried out as sharp pain radiated up her leg.

He reached out to help stabilize her. She took several breaths and managed a smile. "Sorry."

His eyebrow shot up. "For what?"

Yeah, she didn't know. For being an idiot and walking with her head down. For not seeing him standing there? For getting shot. "I don't know, it was a stupid thing to say." And fell silent.

Thankfully he let it go. "Ready?"

She nodded and took a step forward. And stopped, shuddering. Why the hell hadn't she taken the pain killers when Cooper had offered? She bit her lip. Now she'd have to wait for them to kick in before she'd feel better.

It was on the tip of her tongue to ask Shadow for help when he scooped her up into his arms. She looped her arms around his neck happily. "You're a good man."

He shook his head. "You have no idea what you're talking about."

"Really? Why, because I'm a woman? Because I'm injured?"

"Because you don't know me," he snapped, his voice harsh.

She stilled and stared up at him. What was going on inside that massive intelligence of his? And why?

"You don't scare me," she whispered, realizing that they had reached the truck. "No matter what you're thinking, you're not bad – you're good. Honorable. Stalwart. Capable."

He slanted her a long look of disbelief.

She beamed up at him. "It's true."

"You're living in that sunny world of yours again."

"I always live there," she said in a low voice as he set her down on the bench seat. "You could come visit me."

He went to back away, but she reached up and tugged his face down toward her and kissed him ever so gently. As she slowly withdrew she added, "You don't have to live in the shadows, maybe it's time to experience a little sunshine for yourself."

SHADOW RETURNED TO the dead man's side. He ignored the grins of his fellow SEALs. They were all idiots. Then, so was he. He didn't even know what to think about Arianna. He felt drawn to her side all the time. He needed to focus on his work, the job at hand, instead he found himself constantly looking at her, to check that she was okay. Be with her. There was a hunger inside he didn't recognize. Not a sexual hunger, although that hummed constantly below the surface too, and that's the part that surprised him. She was gorgeous and he'd do pretty damn much anything to take her to bed, but there was something else going on inside. This need, this wish to be with her, to under-stand her view and her life that she kept giving him little glimpses off. It was…different. He hadn't seen it right away. Then the circumstances were hardly normal. Then he'd thought she might have been joking about the sunshine and rainbows, but she really seemed to be like that, and he didn't get it. Didn't understand how it could be. She'd not had such a perfect life that she'd only seen the good in life. She'd been born unique, special, and somehow that part of her had survived the trauma called life.

He grinned at the phrasing. He didn't really believe growing up and surviving this world was a trauma. Neither did he believe anyone survived unscathed. But whereas most people might walk through life and hide away the hurts and hide away from those who hurt them, Arianna had this sunny, that's okay I know it won't happen again attitude.

It was likely to reach around and bite her in the ass sometime soon.

"So, buddy, that's quite the facial expression. Kind of like you don't know what hit you and not sure what to do with the blow," Dane said in a low voice. "You okay?"

Not wanting to get into anything personal – like hell he was going to discuss any of this – Shadow nodded. "Fine."

"Right. So you're not but you don't want to discuss it. Got it."

And Dane gave him a mock salute and with a smile he walked toward Mason who was on his phone trying to make arrangements to collect the body.

Shadow studied Dane. He'd been struck by lightning on one of their trips. Been completely sideswiped by meeting Marielle and had been pretty grumpy about it for a while too. But he'd walked forward regardless, and now he was so damn happy it was sickening.

And made Shadow realize just how possible this all was.

Maybe.

Arianna might like Shadow as a rescuer – but as a man? That didn't mean there was anything more to it than simple attraction.

Shadow had been seriously disappointed in his life. He knew exactly how easy it was to *not* get what he wanted in this world, so he'd made it easier on himself by choosing to *not* want much. He kept his life simple now. Straightforward.

Until he hit a wall called Arianna.

Now he knew there was something he really wanted and most likely couldn't have. So he could go for it and possibly have his hopes dashed or not bother because he knew the outcome already.

He studied the interior of the store while his mind was already busy tracking the events of what had gone on, almost like a weird psychic ability, his mind could put the pieces together and show him what had happened. The store owner, living out where he did, had likely been too talkative on a day the kidnappers couldn't afford to talk to anyone. They'd taken the simple route.

And he'd gotten a bullet for being friendly.

Too bad he couldn't get Arianna to learn the same lesson. She was going to get seriously hurt one day.

Swede stepped in front of him with a determined look on his face as Shadow tried to refocus on their next step.

Shadow frowned. "What?"

"You're not going to break that girl's heart are you?"

"Of course not." He gave Swede a good frown. "She's not in any danger of having it broken."

Swede shook his head. "Don't be so blind to something special right in front of your nose that you hurt your chances at happiness because you think she's better off without you."

That made him step back mentally. Outside he narrowed his gaze at his best friend and warned him to back off.

The problem with Swede was now that he'd found happiness he wanted to see everyone around him happy. Well, given that only Shadow and Cooper were still single on the team... "Go tell that to Cooper," he snapped.

"She's not interested in Cooper," Swede said calmly. "Although he might be interested if you aren't."

"I thought you said she wasn't interested." Shadow could feel his shoulders hunching in on themselves. He hated this stuff. And never did heart to heart – especially not with his buddies.

"If he's there for her, and you've turned her away, then she just might head in that direction. It's natural to go where you are wanted. She can only keep butting up against the rejection for so long before she turns to another for comfort."

His gut twisted.

"You're gonna have to make a decision soon."

"No decision to make. She's a senator's daughter and sees me as her rescuer. Like anyone in her situation, she's grateful."

Swede studied him for a long moment. "And you don't want gratitude, is that it?"

Shadow shot him a hooded look. "Would you?"

"Nope. But I think you're wrong. I think Arianna doesn't give a shit about where you are from, or your lineage or lack of it, or that you saved her ass a couple of times, she saved yours a time or two as I recall, I don't see you bending over with gratitude…" Swede crossed his arms. "I do however think she sees something in you that you don't see yourself."

Shadow had already turned to join the others. At Swede's words, he froze. Slowly, he turned back to face his friend. "What is that?"

He hated that he could hear that tiny bit of hope weaving through his voice. But it was there damn it. Swede would know. He missed nothing. Shadow had been off his mark since he'd met Arianna. Like what was with that? He couldn't let her distract him so much but thoughts of her filled his mind. Wouldn't let go.

Swede walked past and reached out to smack him on the shoulder. "You'll have to figure that out yourself."

And he refused to say any more.

CHAPTER 14

ARIANNA LAY DOWN on the back of the truck, her leg throbbing. Shit. It was better then worse, with the worse part building. She still hadn't gotten more pain medicine. And she was getting weepy. Was there anything worse?

She already felt so damn female when surrounded by all these macho men. And weepy just seemed to go along with being hurt. She wanted to be strong and capable beside them. Hated to think she was doing her sex an injustice. That all the women in the world were looking at her like she'd let them down. Everything had been good until she got hurt.

Cooper's head popped over the back seat of the truck. She wasn't even startled. There were so many men in and out and around always looking after her she never knew who it would be next.

"You okay?"

She nodded but didn't open her eyes. "Yeah."

"Liar. The leg is killing you, isn't it?"

Her lips twisted and she stared up at him. He was seriously gorgeous. Friendly. An all–around nice guy. So why couldn't she be hooked on him instead of Shadow. Shadow's darkness called to her. Reached into the deepest part of her and wrapped her heart up in caring and warmth. If only she could do the same for him and wrap his heart up in a loving hug.

Cooper shook out two pills from a bottle and handed them to her, along with a sealed bottle of water. He popped the top as she sat up. She stared at the pills. "I really hate that these help."

"No point in being in pain if you don't have to be. Your body needs rest. It can't heal if it's fighting the pain. We got to do what we got to do. And healing that leg is important. I wish we had antibiotics for it."

Shadow appeared at the truck. "We've got an antibiotic cream from the store for those scratches of yours though." He held it up, adding, "It's not much but it's something and we need to change that dressing too."

He disappeared then reappeared with a small medical kit. Cooper shifted back out of the front of the cab. "Let me know if you need any help."

She stared at Shadow and then the kit and realized what he meant, and her whole body cringed at the thought. "Oh no, Shadow, please not."

That stare of his didn't change. Her lower lip trembled. She took a deep breath, feeling the shudder of fear ripple throughout her whole body and regardless of the pain killers she'd just taken her leg started to boom in earnest.

"Sorry, Arianna," he said. "It's got to be done."

She sniffled back the pleas under her tongue. She knew it did. But she didn't want it to happen at all, didn't want them to think less of her.

She rolled onto her back, wincing as her leg was jarred, and crossed her arms over her chest. "Okay, I'm ready."

His regretful sigh filled the truck. At least he wasn't looking forward to this process either.

In fact, he was so gentle…it surprised her. Her pants were lowered to her ankles, like how embarrassing, and the bandage cut away from her leg. When he lifted the dressing off her skin, she was watching his face, trying to gauge his reaction to her wound.

When he didn't say anything, she whispered, "How bad is it?"

"Surprisingly good," he said and glanced up at her. "Are you going to look at it?"

That's when she realized she'd squeezed her eyes closed. She shook her head. "Nope. It's going to hurt more if I do."

"So if you ignore things they don't hurt you?"

She heard the humor in his voice and realized how silly that sounded. Right. Along with so much else of her attitude and outlook in the world. "It might be silly to you, but if it helps me get through this, then it's working fine."

Silence. Not that she cared. She was so focused on not blubbering like a baby this time she barely noticed. Besides, it was getting harder to sense that silence through the rest of the noise. The rest? Damn. She winced inside as she realized the other noise *was* her blubbering like an idiot. Tears pouring down her cheeks and she sniffed like a two-year-old. She'd always been a baby to pain. And here he most likely hadn't even started cleaning her leg. How totally unheroic of her. So much for wanting to make a good impression. She was acting the same as ever.

Well, it was for the better. Guys like Shadow didn't want watering pots like herself. She swiped at her eyes and tried to turn off the waterworks. It took a long moment before she mustered up the courage to peek out from under her lashes. He was likely disgusted with her.

Instead, he stood outside the truck and stared at her with such an odd look on his face. A look that said he didn't know what to do with her. Well, she didn't know what to do with him either.

But what if that look was about her leg? Maybe he'd lied earlier.

"Is it bad?" she whispered struggling to sit up. "Tell me the truth."

Immediately he shook his head. "No, your wounds are doing quite well." Then he shrugged and added, "At least as well as can be expected."

She frowned. "That means it's doing terrible."

He gave her a long look. "I said it was doing well, didn't I?"

"Sure." She struggled to sit, bracing herself for fresh tears when the pain hit, but was surprised to find that although it was aching and sore, it wasn't screaming at her. "But then you couched in terms that meant it would do better under different circumstances?"

"Sure, if you were in a bed and not trying to walk and had maybe a dose of antibiotics in you so as to not be in danger of getting an infection, you know...ideal circumstances. But you aren't, so given that you aren't, you're doing fine."

She blinked as she tried to process what he was saying. Then gave it up. It sounded reassuring and she was willing to trust him.

Besides, she needed something else from him. And he wasn't going to give it to her unless he knew she needed it. And he, big oaf that he was, wasn't going to know unless she told him. Only she didn't want to have to. "I'd be a lot better if I had one more thing," she announced expectantly.

"What's that?"

She gave him a big smile. Surely he'd be able to guess. "I'm sure you can figure it out if you put your mind to it."

There was that so very predictable frown. With a quick shake of his head, he said, "No, what do you need."

She sighed and wiggled to the open passenger door so her leg could hang down. Then she opened her arms. Immediately, he stepped forward to help her out of the truck.

Idiot. Sure enough he stepped back as soon as she was standing.

She shook her head. "No. That's not what I needed."

At his confused look, she motioned for him to lean down. When he promptly did so, she whispered. "I need a hug, please."

Instantly, he cuddled her close. Oh happy sigh. It's not that he didn't want to, or that he wasn't willing, he just wasn't much of a toucher and that was too bad, he was so, so good at it. She let out a big sigh and smiled up at him. He stared down at her, an unreadable look on his face. She smiled. "It's okay. I'll keep your secret."

His eyebrows shot up and a worried look crossed his face. "And what secret is that?"

"You're an awesome hugger." She reached up and kissed his cheek.

He shook his head, once again not sure what to do with her easy affection "What was that for?"

"As a thank you." Her grin deepened, her irrepressible good humor surfacing. "For letting me cry like a baby."

That brought a grin to his face. "You did much better this time."

"Right, sure I did." She rolled her eyes at his nice comment.

"At least you're allowing me to save face. And the others?" She looked around and at not seeing anyone she added only half joking, "Did I scare them away with my bawling."

"You didn't bawl," he said seriously. "You were quiet and tears are allowed. You're hurt and hurting and sometimes tears are the only answer. Don't be so hard on yourself."

His words surprised her but so did the warm caring way he delivered them. Much happier, she leaned against his chest just happy to be held. She wasn't clingy usually but she did love being close to him.

"Besides, most of the men have gone to find someone to talk to from the town."

"Hopefully, they found lots of people." She glanced around. "I can't imagine something like this being ignored." And that was another reminder. She tilted her head back. "Still no word on my family?"

He shook his head. She sighed. "How am I getting home at this point?"

"Waiting on orders to answer that."

Her lips curled. "If they are as good at making decisions as the rest of the government it will be Christmas before we get a solid answer."

He grinned. "True enough. But we're heading back to California and you're supposed to go to...where, Oregon?"

She shook her head. "We live in Newport Beach, CA."

"Really?" His tone held more than surprise in it.

She nodded. "Why?"

He was silent for a long moment then said, "I live at the base. Coronado."

She gave him a fat grin. They didn't live that far apart. She'd love to see him after this mess was over. But he had a life there. "I guess you'll be happy to go home."

"Always, but that doesn't change the fact that I'll likely be called out in another day or week or month."

"Always something needing your attention. My father would say the same for him."

The two smiled.

"What do you do for a living," he asked her. "Our files didn't include much about you."

"What, not my education, favorite foods, past lovers, or the color of my underwear?" she asked in a mocking voice. "Who knew?"

"Pink."

She stared up at him in confusion.

"The color of your underwear is pink. You went to UCLA but I don't think the program you started in is the one you completed and you've had past lovers but not the right ones."

Oh boy. She tried to close her gaping mouth but it was damn hard. She *was* wearing pink panties, and he had no choice but to see them considering he'd removed her pants to clean her leg wound—twice. That he noticed brought a flush to her cheeks. But as for the rest... Oddly enough her mind latched onto the one thing he'd missed and the easier topic to carry forward. "And my favorite food?" she challenged, still trying to figure out what his comment about not having the right lovers meant.

He slanted her a devastatingly cute sideways grin that had her heart racing instantly and said, "Chocolate of course."

"Damn."

He laughed. "So what field of study did you complete?"

With a resentful look his way she said, "I'm a teacher. My father wanted me to be a lawyer and follow his footsteps but..." She looked away. "I just couldn't."

"Of course not. You'd want to give the victim everything and be devastated when the victim turned out to not be a victim," he said promptly.

"Well, something like that." She wrinkled up her nose at him. "I just couldn't do that type of work. It wasn't me," she said, staring back at the long years of fighting with her father. "Father never understood."

"Of course not. First you were female and second you're a bleeding heart," he said, but the words were so full of warm laughter it took the sting out.

"Not in all things," she protested. "I also don't get along well with my father or my stepmother."

"Why would you? They are the opposite of you, aren't they? They give money because it's expected of them, a requirement of their social status and to make sure that they attend the most public of functions so that everyone knows they did their duty. You on the other hand probably give money to the local animal shelter and hand over money to the single moms and old folks in the area."

"Food. I take food to the old folks in my building. And shop for them sometimes," she said. "My father threatened to cut off my allowance when he found out I was doing that as a teen." She sighed at the memories.

"And what did you do then?" he asked.

"I told him to go ahead and I'd be sure to contact the local newspaper about the senator who cut off the support for those less fortunate," she confessed.

He nudged her chin up and searched her eyes.

"See," she whispered, needing him to see her as she really was. "I'm not a very nice person."

His lips twitched. "Sweetie, the world I live in – you're a pink puff ball full of niceness."

She blinked then narrowed her gaze at him. Was he mocking her? Hadn't he understood what she'd said? "I don't think you understand," she said earnestly. "I took advantage of the situation."

He snickered. "No, you did what you had to do."

Now she was getting mad. "No I didn't. I could have walked away and not said anything to him. But I was upset and angry."

But he wasn't listening. "You were not a bad person for what you did."

"I blackmailed him," she snapped. "Weren't you listening?"

Mason's cold voice cut through the conversation. "Who did you blackmail and does it relate to this case."

That did it, Shadow burst out laughing.

Arianna reached out and plowed her fist into his belly. The rest of the men crowded around. She couldn't figure out if they were stunned that she'd hit him or the fact that Shadow was damn near rolling on the ground in hysterics.

"You...you..." And words failed her.

The men were helpful though.

"Meanie," Dane suggested.

"Arrogant SOB," said Hawk helpfully.

"Asshole," said Cooper with a huge grin.

"No, I couldn't call him that," she said with a gasp. "But he is a meanie. And hurtful. And not very accepting of my faults."

That did it. The others started to snigger and Shadow fell on his butt to the ground, holding his head in his hands as he tried to stop the laughter rolling through him.

She stared at them and then at him. "Why won't he believe me?"

Mason, his voice desperately trying to quell the humor, said, "Then explain and we'll pass judgment."

She blinked at him suspiciously. The others were trying to calm down so they could hear. She sighed and quickly explained. She finished with, "So I blackmailed my father into continuing my allowance. See... I told Shadow here I was a terrible person, and he should find someone much better than me."

The men, huge grins on their faces all nodded. She wailed. "You all think I'm terrible too."

And damn if her lower lip didn't tremble.

Mason, once again the voice of reason said, "And after you blackmailed your father, what did he do?"

"He doubled the amount," she said with a small grin.

"And just for the record," Shadow said from the ground where Swede was offering a helping hand. "You never said I should find someone better than you."

"Oh, so you want to repeat that in front of all your friends? Just to humiliate me more."

He sighed.

"Look, they are laughing at me," she lamented.

He groaned. "They aren't laughing at you, they're laughing at me."

"What?" she turned to face all the men who were grinning or trying to hide grins but still nodding their heads. "You wouldn't..."

She spun so she was standing in front of Shadow, defending

him, her feistiness rising to the surface. "You can't laugh at him, he's your friend. He's a good man."

"Oh for the love of Go–"

"Now what?" she cried out, turning to face him. "I can't have them making fun of you. That's not nice. Everyone thinks you're cold and mean. They don't know you like I do. You're a marshmallow inside."

"Marshmallow?" Swede asked in a barely controlled voice.

"Softie is probably good," Hawk suggested helpfully.

"I like the pussycat term she used before," Dane said. "Yeah, that's really a good description of Shadow."

"Exactly," she said earnestly, spinning to beam at the men. "Inside he's really a lovable person, even if he often shows a cold, detached exterior."

"Jesus," Shadow said and jerked her around and into his arms. "Enough already. You're killing my hard earned reputation."

She opened her mouth again to blast him, but he calmly picked her up. "Remember how I shut you up last time?"

And he kissed her. Again.

HE HAD TO stop doing that.

The rest of his team were cheering him on and he felt like a heel. Pulling back he studied the slumberous look she gave him. His lips tilted. She didn't appear to be bothered by the crowd around them. He'd hate for her to feel they didn't respect her because they did – if for no other reason than for taking him on.

Crack.

Shadow hit the ground, pulling Arianna over with him. He

heard her cry of pain and hoped to hell it was because of her original injury and not a second bullet. He'd deliberately pulled her on top of him as he fell, but now he rolled, tucking her under the vehicle and came up, gun out and ready. His team had scattered, Cooper crouched beside him swearing in low tones but the language he used, yeah the air had turned ripe. There was blood on his shoulder, but it was only a scratch. Thank heavens, Cooper had just gotten back to Active Duty, he'd be pissed to be sidelined so quickly.

He peered around the grill of the truck. Mason had managed to get to the far side of the gas pumps, not the ideal location but he could maneuver around behind the neighbor's house if he got cover.

And Shadow could give him that. Catching his eye, they set up the timing and on the count of three, Shadow jumped up and started firing. When Mason was safe, Shadow popped back down and looked at Arianna. She lay quietly where he'd placed her, her gaze locked on him and huge.

He gave her a reassuring smile. "It's okay."

But her look said she didn't believe him. And considering more firepower was being exchanged she had good reason.

"Shadow…"

The hiss came from the store behind him. Dane was there, motioning at him to join him.

"Cooper," he said in an urgent whisper. "I'm taking her inside the store."

"Got it."

With a warning glance at Arianna, Shadow scooped her up in his arm and raced to the store and inside as Cooper covered them.

"Do we have any idea who or how many?" he asked when he came to a stop inside. Arianna had looped her arms around his head.

"No. Two for sure."

"Same group?" Shadow asked. He looked at the back door, in his mind he could see the layout of the other houses. And the distance he'd have to travel to reach safety.

"That amount of shooting I'm going to say yes." Dane motioned to the back. "Swede took off and went to the left, Hawk went to the right."

"Cooper is at the truck and Mason at the pumps," Shadow added filling him in. "Now Arianna is here."

"Keep an eye on her," Shadow said. He carefully lowered her to beside a wall full of ropes and other miscellaneous items. "I'll be back," he whispered.

At the next round of gunfire he bolted out the back door.

CHAPTER 15

ARIANNA HUDDLED IN the corner of the store, arms over her head as the gunfire rained all around the building. Shots hit the old wooden structure but didn't penetrate the thick walls. Smoke filled the air, making it difficult to breathe, but she honestly couldn't figure out if that was the panic or residue in the air. When there appeared to be a small break in the shooting, she slowly lowered her arms. And froze.

The smell hit her at the doorway. The storekeeper lay on the floor in front of her. She hadn't seen him before. Now the dead man came clearly into view. He'd been covered with an old plaid hunting shirt but laid up against the back of the counter. She had no doubt about his identity. The poor man.

"Arianna?" Dane's harsh whisper broke her out of her reverie.

"I'm here. I'm fine."

"Good."

"What's going on out there? Surely that's more than one man?"

"Yeah, looks like three."

Three. She shook her head. "Did the other prisoners get away from the soldiers and somehow come into town via a different route?"

"We didn't see a different route. Mason has been trying to contact the other soldiers. We could use the backup, and if they are traveling toward us, we don't want them to get caught in the trap."

"No, there're enough dead men already." Too many dead. Thankfully most of the deaths hadn't involved her.

She didn't count the guy she knocked out of the tree. He'd been going after her brother. Kevin. Thank God her brother wasn't here with her now. That would be terrible for him. He should be home safe and sound. But with both parents injured and in the hospital she had no idea where he'd go. Who'd look after him? He'd be with her if she'd gone home. If she was allowed to leave. Her leg didn't feel horrible but neither did it feel terrific. The hospital might have sent her home to heal or they'd have forced her to wait in the hospital a day or two longer. And Kevin would be in the same boat as he was now.

At least he'd escaped without physical injury, but she knew these past events would scar him for life. How could it not? He was a strong boy though and with help he'd get past this.

She just wished she was there with him now.

The silence outside continued in an elongated moment. She twisted to look up at Cooper. "Any idea what's happening out there?"

"No. Not yet. If our team can sneak up and take them out, this could be over in minutes."

"Or hours," she muttered.

"Hopefully not. We aren't into sieges."

"Good." As the words left her mouth a short burst of gunfire sounded behind the store. Shit. She'd feel better if that had been out front.

Cooper raced to hide behind the door. Arianna scrunched up as small as she could.

Slowly the door was pushed open and swung loose. No hand visible. Nobody walking inside. Her breath caught in the back of her throat, and she pressed harder against the shelves at her back. Now what the hell...

A man somersaulted inside, and with guns blazing, he spun and fired. She lay flat on the floor as the bullets rained over her head.

A single shot fired.

The gunman collapsed to the floor, a bullet between the eyes. Shadow walked inside the store, kicked the gun away from the dead man and nudged him with his boot. Satisfied the danger had been neutralized, he turned to study Arianna. "Cooper," he called out.

"Yep," Cooper said, "Right behind you."

"Anyone else in here," Shadow asked in a dark, flat voice that left Arianna breathless at the dangerous man in front of her.

"Only us," she whispered. "And now two dead guys."

He shifted to the window. "Mason took out one, this is two. We're looking for at least one more. Maybe two more. We're afraid they've holed up in one of the houses, possibly holding a family hostage."

"To what purpose," Cooper asked. "They failed in their mission. What's the point of attacking innocent bystanders?"

"No idea. They might have been holding them as insurance for the senator as extra leverage."

"Makes no sense," Arianna said. "If his own family didn't do it, a house of strangers wouldn't either."

"I have to agree," Shadow said. "It could have been insurance in case their group got into trouble."

"Or to persuade you to hand me over?"

Shadow shot her a hard look. "Not happening."

"I think once the plan blew up and they lost three family members, they realized the senator wasn't going to do what they wanted, so they looked to grab me to save something of the operation. Or maybe they needed me as extra insurance to gain their freedom." She shuddered. "You have to help the family."

"We are planning to. But that's not going to work out so well if we can't shut down the men hunting us." He spun around and crept to the open door. "First things first."

And once again he disappeared.

She looked from the second dead man to Cooper. "Do you want to go after Shadow?"

Cooper shook his head. "Shadow operates on a whole different level than the rest of us. He works best alone."

She nodded, trying not to worry about the man. If he was the best then he was doing what he needed to do. She glanced over at the killer's gun. "Can you give me his gun?" She pointed to the assault rifle Shadow had kicked against the far wall. "I don't want to be defenseless."

"It's not a beginner's weapon," Cooper said cautiously. "You could kill all of us with that thing."

She stared at it with misgivings. "I wouldn't want to hurt you... But I don't want to be a sitting duck for the next man either."

Cooper carefully closed the door part way and picked up the rifle. He checked it over then walked toward her. "I've put the safety on. If you click this," and he showed her, "then it's basically point and shoot. But you need to have a target in sight and it's going to fire multiple rounds as soon as you pull this trigger."

"Oh." She carefully looked at the mean looking weapon and realized she wanted nothing to do with it. Particularly if she did something wrong. Taking a deep breath, she said, "Take it away. I don't want it."

She ignored the relief on his face.

But she could understand how he felt. She didn't want to be caught unarmed, but if she were armed and someone approached they'd kill her anyway. She'd be the one hesitating to pull the trigger so she'd be just as dead.

SHADOW'S HEART HAD damn near seized up when he saw the gunman sneaking around the side of the door. Too hidden for a clear shot, too far away for a tackle and too damn close to Arianna. Shadow was already on the run when the man had disappeared into the store. With the gunshots filling the air, he burst through to see the gunman lining up a shot. He couldn't see a target but there were only two choices and neither were ones he was prepared to lose.

He fired one shot to the head. The man fell and never moved again.

Thank God. But this was so not over. With relief coursing through his veins he'd raced back outside and to the house on the north end of town. The faster he traveled, the more he considered her theory. Would they be looking for hostages to get out of the country? With the resources available to them, surely they could have slipped away without this. He had to wonder if anyone lived here. Or was this place a ghost town. Then again, the store owner lived here. But there'd been nothing fresh in the store. So he didn't cater to locals as much as travelers, and there couldn't be many of them through here. The roads led to nowhere. Just more roads north. There wasn't any major center further past the cabin and the road into that place hadn't been traveled in many years. Mother Nature had tried to reclaim most of it.

The team had checked the south end of town already. There were four houses there. Two were derelict and empty. The other two vacant but in better shape. Now they were heading to the houses they'd passed on their drive in to town.

He moved and shifted with the changing landscape, blending in and out as required. In the distance he heard a dog bark. Then nothing. That wasn't normal. He shifted back a few steps and changed his angle. The dog barked again. Good. Dogs made great warning systems for both those he protected and predators. They let them know what the dog was sensing at what time. People never thought of that. Shadow caught sight of Swede two houses up. He motioned at Shadow to come closer.

Keeping low and moving fast, he quickly joined Swede.

"Hawk and Mason are on the other side." He pointed to the last house. "If there are more shooters here, they have to be inside this one."

"Where's the dog?"

Swede shook his head. "No idea. Haven't seen one."

Shadow frowned. "If it's not there, it's got to be somewhere close as I heard one. And dog means people."

"We haven't found more. But…" he motioned to the woods. "There could be more in there."

Shadow studied the thick trees that completely blocked any

view of what was behind. "I'm going to scout that area."

"You're worried about the dog?"

"Yes, because he's not alone." And Shadow headed for the woods.

CHAPTER 16

S HE HATED TO sit and wait. There had to be something she could do. Something useful. The other military unit would be joining them soon – surely she could help the process of ending this mess somehow. She slid over to the dead kidnapper and struggled to remove his wallet from his pants.

Cooper, always on guard, asked, "What did you find?"

"His ID."

"Really?" He motioned at her. "Toss it to me."

She'd already done a quick search and hadn't found anything else. She flung it lightly in his direction and it was more due to his skill than hers that he caught it. She went back to searching the rest of the man's pockets. She didn't recognize his face but figured based on the khaki outfit he was part of the same kidnapper group. God help her if they ever decided to change those uniforms.

In the last chest pocket she found something harder and crumpled.

She pulled it out and gasped in shock. It was a picture of her standing outside her own condo.

"What is it?"

She struggled to reorient herself. Such a horrid thing to find but maybe not all that unusual given that she'd been on the trip.

She used the checkout counter to pull herself to her feet and held out the picture for Cooper.

He studied it.

"It was taken outside my house," she said. "I know they already kidnapped my family and that's over and done with, but it's a little disturbing to know they were stalking me at home beforehand."

"Maybe and maybe not. They could be using this image to identify you as they know you're the one that didn't get on the plane." He nodded as if liking his hypothesis. "Explains why they are making a play for you here."

"They don't need me now," she exclaimed. "They never did." She shook her head. "Could these men have been here since yesterday?" She frowned. "Waiting for their team to show up? Then when we got here instead, all hell broke loose?"

As if the world had heard her, gunshots split the air again. "Oh God," she whispered. "I need this to be over?"

"Soon," he said standing right beside her, both of them peering out the window from the side. "At least it should be."

He turned to look at her. "They might have been using the town as a base. That makes the most sense."

It did. It also meant this wasn't over. The continuous shooting worried her. She'd known Shadow was safe when she'd seen him here, but with this new round... What if he'd been shot?

She hobbled toward the door.

"Whoa, where are you going?"

She waved her hand outside. "I wanted to look around."

"Bad idea," he said. "We wait until they come back."

"Aren't you getting tired of being the babysitter?"

He laughed. "Sure, but I was off active duty for a long time due to a bad injury, so I'm just damn happy to be back as much as I am." His grin widened. "If that's being your babysitter – no worries. I've had worse jobs."

She tried to study him covertly but couldn't see any physical injury on him. So whatever had happened, he'd healed. "I suppose they want to keep you safe as much as possible too."

His grin widened. "I doubt that's the reason as much as everyone wants in on the action, only someone has to stay behind."

"So you drew the short straw." She laughed at his look. "That's okay. I'm happy to have you with me."

"My pleasure," he said simply. "You're a special woman."

The glance she sent him said he was out of his mind. "I'm an idiot. I could have had an easy life but no, that wasn't good enough for me."

"I thought you were a lawyer. Or started as one."

"Sure, but before then my daddy tried to marry me off to a judge." She winced at the memory. "Told me it was the best he could do for me. And I should take the offer as I wasn't likely to get a better one."

There was an awkward silence. "And how old was this judge?"

"Early fifties I think. Back then that seemed ancient. I was in the last term of high school."

"Wow. Nice father."

"He is in many ways, but he has strong views on a woman's place. It's because of him I applied to law school. No one was more surprised than I was when I got in. But it was the wrong place for me."

He stayed quiet for a bit, then said, "Your father was also at an advanced age when he started a family."

"True enough. And even older when he fathered Kevin and yes, he is the father of us both. Insisted on DNA tests." She smiled. "He is consistent."

"Interesting. Maybe an effect of his career. Maybe his age."

"And the way he was reared by an older father himself. He didn't have my father until he was sixty–five himself."

Cooper's eyebrows shot up. "Wow. That would have an impact, I'm sure."

She nodded. "I don't blame my father, but it has made me head in the opposite direction. He's dark so I'm light. He's serious so I'm not. He's all about image…" She grinned. "And I'm not. As you can see. My father's clothes were the top casual for the man–at–the–cabin look he could buy." She motioned to her oversized black sweatpants. "And I'm wearing Shadow's pants and damn glad to have them," she admitted. "I think the biggest thing was he's all about image so I'm all about real." She sighed and leaned against the wall. "It's hard though as my mother was a watering pot and ditzy to boot. And I have way too much of that in me."

"No, you don't. You temper it with courage and independence and caring. You have to be yourself and given the two different people you came from, I think you did a wonderful job."

She grinned, feeling chipper in spite of everything. "Now tell me that Shadow believes the same thing you do, and you'll have made my day."

"Oh my broken heart," he said in a mocking tone. "You shot a single arrow and killed me with that comment."

"Nah, you might be interested in me but you're not *interested* in me."

His dancing eyes landed on her. "Even if I was, Shadow is the man in your heart and that guy deserves to have someone sweet in his world."

"Aw. That's so nice of you to say." She beamed up at him. "Now if only he'd get that message, too."

"I'd tell him but he needs to figure it out for himself."

She nodded seriously. "So true. And as I suspect that he'd be one of the last to go down in the line of fire, I think he'd be the same in terms of letting down the guards to his heart."

"But that doesn't mean you should give up…" he said in alarm.

"Oh, I won't give up," she said with a smile. "But I might just have to change tactics."

And she wouldn't say any more.

THE TREES WERE so thick and stick thin Shadow could barely make his way through the woods. The place was in need of a controlled burn before Mother Nature took care of it herself. The undergrowth was strewn with old broken sticks and dead leaves. Treacherous for walking and deadly to try and sneak up on anyone. He'd skirted the worst of the area and now peered down what appeared to be a dirt driveway. There were tracks at least. He slipped from tree to tree working his way deeper into the woods until it finally opened up to show a log cabin at least forty years old. Untreated, the logs had long ago turned grey.

There was a fenced yard with a dog run along the back. He could hear the snarling sound of canines fighting over territory. So there was at least one, if not two. But where were the owners? He'd have expected the kidnappers to shoot the dogs first. Unless something else was going on here. Then again shooting the dogs let the neighbors know something was up. Shadow quickly traced the perimeter.

There were no lights inside. No vehicles outside but a garage or workshop sat on the far corner of the property. He worked his way over to the back of the small outbuilding. There were windows but no lights. There was, however, a back door. He turned the knob. The door unlatched. Inside, he could see nothing but a row of white. His eyes slowly adjusted to add hair and glowing eyes to the row of teeth in the darkness. But the guard dog never made a sound.

Shadow closed his eyes and reached out to the dog mentally like he'd done many times before. All animals responded to him well but the wilder ones even more so. They might have seen him as an equal, not competition. He didn't know, but they generally had little argument over his presence.

Still, there was always going to be that one instance where the rule didn't hold true. He hoped it wasn't this one. The dog looked well cared for except there was blood on his haunch. His own or someone else's? He took a step toward the animal, speaking in a low voice. As he approached, the dog curled back his lip and showed fangs. Shadow stopped and searched for food. Behind the one dog, lay a second one. Injured. Or dead. Oh, crap. He shouldered his rifle and walked closer as if he had the right. The dog had been raised by people and likely a gun had been responsible for the injury. The dog growled deeper but let him pass. He crouched down beside the injured dog and gently ran a hand over the older lab cross. She was dead. A bullet square in her ribs. She'd not had a chance. Bastards. He hated anyone killing animals unless for food, and when it was a pet like this one—well there was no excuse.

Slowly, Shadow turned to the other dog, "I'm sorry, boy. She's gone." At the sound of his voice, the dog lay down and dropped his nose on his paws. And whimpered.

Shadow gently stroked the young animal's head. "You already knew that though, didn't you? Sorry, buddy. There's a lot of pain going on around here right now."

He gave a quick search to the garage and found a truck parked on the side. He walked over. The engine was still warm. He popped the hood and pulled off the distributor cap. At least no one would be running away in this rig.

With a final glance at the dog, he quietly closed the door and left. The dog was safer inside right now. But he'd be sure to open the door before he left the property.

The house stood before him. Still no lights or sounds. He raced across the short distance until his back was up against the wall. He listened intently. Still quiet. There were a few basement windows, dusty and caked in dirt. He doubted they'd been cleaned in years. If the windows would open, he could get in that way. But if they were as unused as they appeared to be he wasn't likely to do so silently.

He slid around to the back of the house and the small porch. Also old and creaky likely, but the door was slightly ajar. He frowned, his senses on alert. A trap or someone in a hurry.

Then he heard it.

A tiny snuffle.

Not a young one either. An older woman with a cold came to mind. The proverbial hankie in her hand. And likely a captor at her side.

She sniffled again.

"Shut the fuck up."

Shadow smiled. Perfect. Now he had a target.

CHAPTER 17

A RIANNA WANDERED THE store feeling useless and hating the wait. Her mind spun endlessly after seeing the photo of herself in that man's pocket. To know someone had been taking photos of her without her knowledge. What a horrible feeling. Especially when she should have been safe now. This mess over and done with. Right? Her family was home safe. Right?

She spun to look at Cooper. "Has anyone had an update on my family?"

There must have been something in the tone of her voice because Cooper turned to her, his glance searching. "We know they arrived at the hospital in San Francisco."

She closed her eyes. "Okay, good. Just for a moment there, given that picture, I was afraid they might have taken my family again."

"We've had confirmation they arrived. We don't have an update on your father's condition, but you already know he's in critical condition and he's not expected to survive the head injuries. Last I heard, your stepmother was recovering."

She nodded. That's what she'd expected. Not easy to deal with given her current circumstances. She'd loved her own father but... For Kevin's sake, she hoped her stepmother survived and was capable of raising Kevin. He needed it. He'd had a cold childhood already. He needed so much more.

She needed to get home to him. "Is someone coming to help out?"

He nodded. "The other military team is on the way. And they have the hostages still. More soldiers are en route to help out." He glanced at his watch. "They should be here soon."

"Then what?"

He shrugged. "Good question. I'm not leading this and we're not on home territory. Quite likely we'll be sent on our way."

She brightened. "Perfect!" She glanced over at the man on the ground. "I wonder what happened to the leader."

"The man you sent the photo of?"

"He said something in passing that he was picking up someone." She shrugged. "I don't know who."

Cooper stared at her. "Interesting."

She nodded. "Maybe if we knew who and where they were we could grab both of them. But that was a long time ago. He's likely halfway around the world by now."

"Could be. Any idea why they targeted your father?"

"Something to do with needing his vote on something major." She studied the man on the floor. "But that made no sense to me. My father has always made his position clear."

"Is he close to anyone else in the House?"

She glanced over at him. "Close, no. Not really. He doesn't socialize with many and when he does it's usually for political or charity functions."

He wandered the store, never losing that alertness inside.

"What are you thinking?"

"Your father is well known to be a hard ass, correct?"

"Correct."

"So what if someone was using him to force other Congressmen to take a stance. Your father is known to never give in. Never break and what's happened to him sends a hell of a message to others."

"I don't understand exactly how the voting works but getting someone else appointed wouldn't be easy."

"But he's not out, is he? As long as he's alive they won't move to change the status any time soon. So in theory if he's used as an example, the others might cave in a lot earlier. You know when you're up against a street gang, if you take out the leader, then the others scatter."

"So you're saying that by taking out my father, the others are more likely to do what they are told to do." She snorted. "Now that could be. I've been tossing this all around in my head and coming up empty."

"We've got a good idea of how this went down but need the details."

"Like?"

"How they knew where you were going, why you were going, when you were going. And how did all of you come together." He walked the few steps toward her. "And we have to consider if there was anyone on the inside."

"Well, it wasn't me," she said with feeling. "The arrangements were made by my father's office. They'd know when and where."

"Anyone else?"

"I don't know who Kevin and Linda might have told but not likely anyone. It was a fast decision. In fact..." She considered the issue. "It was too fast."

"No warning."

"No, I wondered about that. I didn't hear about it until early in the week. And as soon as I did…" She peered out the window but didn't see anything but her memories. "I invited myself." She studied the dead man again. "And as that's the case, why would he have my photo?"

"Maybe you invited yourself, but it's also possible you were going to be forced to go regardless. They could have easily kidnapped you and held you somewhere else."

"I can't understand what makes people do things like this."

"Money and power." He held out the picture to her. "Any idea when this might have been taken?"

She glanced over at it. "I'm wearing the same coat I always wear so that could have been anytime."

"It's in the evening."

"Is it? Then that narrows it down as I don't wear that coat out for any evening functions. It's more for going for a walk or to pick up a few groceries."

"So when would that have been?" he persisted.

She looked at the image again. And saw her neighbor in one of her Old Russian day dresses she always wore. The old woman had passed away a couple of weeks ago. "I can say it's at least three weeks old," she explained.

"And did you know about the plans three weeks ago?"

"No," she said in surprise. "I only heard about it on Monday. We flew out on Friday."

"For the long weekend?"

She nodded. "It was a short holiday and a rather long flight. I think that was my stepmother's biggest issue. But then you have to understand, if a longer vacation was planned, she'd have bitched about it as well. She didn't like to travel."

"But your father insisted?"

She cast her mind back. "I don't know," she admitted. "I was never involved in the discussion." She clenched her fingers into a fist. "I only heard from Kevin that she hadn't wanted to come."

"Any reason to believe she'd be involved?"

Her head shot up and stared. "No. Why would she be?"

"Who inherits?"

That caught her by surprise. "I don't know," she said slowly, not liking his line of questioning. "Likely my stepmother. There should be something there for Kevin's education as well. My father is very wealthy, but I don't know what's in the will."

"What happens if all of you die except Kevin?"

Her stomach started to bubble with an overload of acid. "I don't know." Lord, she hadn't wanted to know. "His guardian would be responsible for him I'm sure."

"And who is that?"

She studied Cooper. "My father's aide. He's been with my father for decades. I've known him all my life. He's my step–uncle, actually," she confessed. "He introduced my father and my stepmother to each other way back when."

SHADOW PUSHED THE back door open with the toe of his boot like a strong wind would. The door swung open soundlessly. About time something worked out. He'd already contacted his team, letting them know where he was and what he was doing.

He slipped inside. And stilled.

The kitchen was empty.

And dark.

He studied the layout, his attention lingering on the chipped teapot and half cup of tea on the table, a single plate with crumbs and a bit of bread left. The decor was dated, unkempt. Not dirty but badly in need of repair. He studied the two doorways into and out of the kitchen. One on the left and one on the right. He shifted to the one furthest away. He could see a living room ahead, but it was dimly lit and held only shelving that he could see. He checked out the room moving silently forward. Whoever lived here had likely been here most of their lives. And had little money or interest in upkeep or modernization. Given the voice and sniffles he'd heard earlier he could see this being a pensioner, likely a widow left alone now and waiting out her last days. He hoped she had someone who cared close by. But given the age of the town and the lack of people living there, he doubted it.

Seeing the room empty and not connecting through to the other side he envisioned it as a parlor from days gone and then closed off later. It was the other side of the house he needed to reach. As he turned back to retrace his steps, he saw a huge cupboard. Weapon in hand, he opened it. And realized it was actually a doorway that matched the old wall panels. It led to the front entrance. He stood and listened. There was only one major room downstairs and whatever was upstairs. He glanced up the old staircase, but there was no way to make it up without alerting whoever was in the house that there was an intruder.

At the entrance to the other room, he could hear an odd sound. His mind raced to catalogue it. And realized it was the sound of someone playing cell phone games. The almost silent sound of the fingers tapping and his soft groans when he missed something and angry breaths as he lost, the muted music as the game played.

Good. Keep the asshole distracted. He slipped around the corner. An old woman huddled on an old dusty couch, her wrists bloodied from the ties on her paper thin skin. She raised her head, her mouth opening to cry out. Shadow placed his finger to his lips. She subsided, shaky but valiant as she glared at the man, dressed in khakis, playing his cell phone.

Shadow raised his rifle.

In a low deadly voice, he said, "Now you have to kidnap old ladies after losing the senator and his family. Is that a demotion?"

At Shadow's first word, the man froze. By the time he'd stopped talking, Shadow was staring into the glittering eyes of one of the kidnappers he recognized from the senator's cabin. So one had escaped and come to warn the men waiting here. Interesting.

"You have two choices. You can stand up and be taken as my prisoner back to Washington or you can reach for that weapon at your side."

The man glared at him. "My death won't matter. Another will take my place. We took money for a job. It must be done."

A spidery tingle shot down Shadow's spine. "Mercenaries. Interesting. We figured you for terrorists."

He shrugged. "We are. But sourcing money is always an issue. Mercenaries bring in good money."

It was and there was a never ending source of assholes who wanted shit done. "And the job?"

He laughed. "It was a double whammy. We got paid for two jobs."

"So tell me…" Shadow said in a conversational voice. "How do two jobs dovetail like that?"

"Some senators needed to make a decision and refused. We were supposed to make an example of Senator Stephenson so the others would cave easier. Beating up that old man felt damn good." He sniggered. "And the other job wanted the old man and the young woman dead. We know the old man isn't going to make it. The young woman, well, if you assholes hadn't rescued her we'd have been in the clear there too."

"And who wanted her dead."

The asshole laughed. "I'm not saying anything more."

Shadow expected as much. "Not a problem. We have a pretty good idea already. It always comes down to money, power or sex."

The man smiled. "Well, it's up to you to figure out which one."

"Not bothered." Shadow motioned to the man's gun. "Kick it over here."

"Nah. You come and get it."

Shadow smiled. "I don't think so." He lifted his rifle butt. "After the men you've murdered I'm totally okay with pulling the trigger right here and now."

The old lady stood up shakily. "He shot my dog," she said, tears in her eyes. "Both of them."

"The old girl didn't make it, but the young one is in the garage and still doing fine."

He heard the old lady's gasp of joy. She struggled to walk past him rubbing her sore wrists. "You be careful," Shadow warned.

"I will," she whispered. "Just please don't let him get away." She shot the stranger a scared look. "He said he'd do me a favor and kill me before he left. That would be an easier death than old age."

The stranger laughed. "Look at you, old and dried up. That's no way…" He scooped up his weapon.

And Shadow shot him.

Dead.

CHAPTER 18

COOPER'S PHONE WENT off. Arianna raced to his side to listen.

"Hey, Shadow. Yes, she's fine."

Arianna beamed. Cooper rolled his eyes at her. "No, I've been taking good care of her. No, I haven't had an update from the others. No, we haven't had anyone else in the store."

When he hung up the phone, Cooper was grinning. "Shadow has taken out one asshole. Now if only we knew how many we were up against."

"No," Mason said in a doorway. "We've taken out four now. Is Shadow on his way back?"

"Yes."

"Good," Mason said. "I just got word the military should be here in an hour to sort this out."

"Are we needed here after that?"

"Only to hand off the operation to them. If they need anything more one or two men can stay behind." Mason studied Arianna. "You're looking better."

"Feeling it too," she said with forced cheerfulness. "More than ready to leave."

He nodded. "Aren't we all?" And he turned and walked back out.

Cooper raised his brows. "Sounds like this one is almost wrapped up."

"I hope so. I just want to go home."

That happened sooner than she expected. With a speed that left her stunned, the military arrived by helicopter. They landed on the edge of town and were followed by a second and third. Soldiers surged through the tiny town, and she could only watch in awe as the military machine took over.

She was quickly helped into one of the helicopters and airborne before she knew it.

Cooper was the only one of the SEALs she saw at the end. She clung to him as they approached the helicopter. "Am I going alone?" she whispered, her eyes darting from one stranger's face to the other, searching for those she knew.

"Yes. They are taking you to the next hospital. You have to get that leg checked. Should have done that hours ago," he said in a reassuring voice.

"I know." She gripped her arms around his neck twice as hard as he loaded her onto the huge black machine. "Doesn't mean I want to go alone."

"If we can, we'll come by. I can't say if we're still needed here or if we'll be sent on our way, but home for us is California."

"Me too." She brightened. "Can they fly me there?"

He shook his head. "No, they can't."

Her face fell. Another soldier motioned at a seat in the helicopter. She swallowed and slowly released her arms from Cooper's neck. Just before he walked way, she called out, "Say good-bye to everyone for me."

He stilled, turned back, and said, "You'll see us again."

"Will I?" she said in a forlorn voice. "It doesn't feel like it."

"I promise."

And he was engulfed in chaos as men ordered him back. The helicopter started up. One soldier hopped up beside her. Seconds later, she was airborne.

It looked like a bad movie as she was slowly lifted above the scene. She watched as the men scurried through every house and a stretcher was brought out for the storekeeper. Too quickly she was too high up to see anything or anyone clearly. She leaned her head back and tried to ignore the man beside her. It wasn't his fault he wasn't the man she wanted beside her. Then, no one was. Was it really over? How could she have connected with Shadow only to lose him at this stage?

"Miss, are you okay?"

She rolled her head to the side, seeing the worry on the soldier's face and tried to smile, realizing that once again a waterfall of tears rolled down her cheeks.

"I'm okay," she managed. "It was a very tough weekend, that's all."

"It's over. You're safe now."

And that was partly why she was crying. Stupid really. Still, she was going to miss those men. All of them. They'd worked their way into her heart in such a way she knew she'd never be able to forget. How could such a crazy weekend happen in the first place and then there was the way it all ended. At that, she started to really cry. The release of stress, the constant danger, the fear, and panic – it had happened in a short time frame. Like a small bomb going off inside, the tears and heartache burst free. The soldier let her cry. She appreciated that. The release was good but made her feel crappy at the same time. How did that work?

They weren't in the air for long before they descended.

The soldier noticed her interest. "We'll be at the hospital in just a few minutes."

She nodded, not caring which hospital. It wasn't the one at home and that's where she wanted to be. But she didn't have time to look at much as soon houses appeared below then a large roof with a landing spot came next. The helicopter lowered gently and landed easily on the spot.

Several people rushed toward her.

She was unloaded onto a stretcher and whisked to a door. Before she was pushed inside, she watched the helicopter rise up and disappear into the clouds above. With it went her dreams of seeing Shadow and his team again. She stared at the long white corridors as she was taken into an elevator and rolled down to the ER. There she was moved into a small curtained off room. She hated everything about it. Not logical, considering they were helping her.

Shadow was already gone, her world lost and empty.

Then the curtain was ripped back. The medical team poured over her as she was partially stripped, her leg poked and prodded, then cleaned. She lay there, vulnerable, as they did what they had to do. Already tired and worn out, she barely reacted.

A doctor leaned over her. "Miss Stephenson, how are you feeling?"

She raised dull eyes to him. "I'm fine. How is my leg?"

He glanced down at it. "It's going to be fine."

"Oh good." She knew it would be. After all, the guys had looked after it. They'd done their best and in this case their best was pretty fine. "Can I go home now?"

"We'll need to keep you for a day or two. Then there's a lot of paperwork to take care of. So should be sometime in the next couple of days."

Paperwork? Who cared about that right now? Without Shadow her world looked so dark and she knew her golden dream attitude wasn't going to pull her out of this one.

But her irrepressible positive thinking latched onto Cooper's promise that they'd see her again. And would try to come by the hospital if they could. Only...what if she was shipped out first? Then what? Then it didn't matter what he said, he'd have done his best and this time it would be that the wheels of bureaucracy had moved too fast. She brightened even more. That never happened. Paperwork...took forever. Right. She'd still be here when the SEALs got free of that town. She had to be...

The doctor stepped back slightly. "Now, there is someone I'd like you to speak with. You've been through a traumatic ordeal. And as you're going to be with us for the next couple of days, I think it would be helpful if you talked to one of our trauma counselors."

She was ready to agree to anything if it meant she could stay until the guys arrived but at his word, *counselor*, she froze.

"Is that like a shrink?" she asked cautiously, her gaze locked on his face. "Surely I don't need that?"

"Don't look at it that way. Dr. Mendelson is very good at her job, and in this case, her job would be to help you get over the horrific experience you've just been through." He straightened and walked to the doorway. "Now that we have that sorted, I'll let her know you're here."

And he was gone.

She stared suspiciously at the doorway, afraid the shrink would be popping through any second. She really didn't want to talk with her, but was it worth fighting over?

She was still mulling it over when an orderly came and raised the bars on her bed. In alarm, she asked, "What are you doing?"

"Not to worry, your room is ready. I'm taking you down." He unclicked the brakes on the wheels and pulled the bed back out slightly. Then unhooked her IV bag to lay it on her bed. "Now we can get you settled in for a pleasant visit. You're only with us for a few days I understand."

He was really nice. Still, part of her was suspicious, was everyone like that here? And then the orderly nudged the curtain accidentally. "Oops, sorry about that. Here I was trying to be so careful."

"It's fine," she said, chuckling inside.

"Well, I'm still sorry. We don't want you to have a bad impression of us."

She counted three more apologies on the way to her room. One when they passed another orderly pushing a different patient in a bed, again as they turned the corner into her room and she moved her hand away even though there was lots of room and then because he couldn't set the bed up any closer to the window. She gave a happy sigh. He was a sweetheart. She was quickly falling in love with the country and the people.

After she was set up in her new bed, a move he made painless, and her IV once again hanging, her medication administered and a wonderful warm blanket wrapped around her, she lay in a haze of wellbeing.

Truly, she was safe now.

And she closed her eyes.

SHADOW MADE HIS way slowly back to the store. Soldiers had arrived at the old woman's house, but it had been Shadow who had dug the grave for the beloved dog and had brought the young one back to the old lady. She'd had tears of gratitude in her eyes as she thanked him again. He'd patted her shoulder, put on the tea kettle, ordered one of the young men who'd arrived to make sure she got a hot cup of tea, had the medical team check her over for other injuries and see if she needed anything else. He made it quite clear that the cupboards were bare and the woman needed more help than a pat on her hand.

The soldier had assured him she'd be taken care of.

Satisfied, Shadow walked back into town watching the military in action as they did a house to house search. His team were standing talking with several military leaders. Good, maybe after the updates they could get back to their original mission. Helicopters had been arriving and leaving steadily. Also good. There were five dead men to take care of. And who knew how many living were in need of medical assistance.

Mason gave him a quick nod as he spoke with the major.

The two men saluted and the major turned to the rest of the team. "You have our thanks, if there is ever anything we can do…"

It wasn't meaningless either. The two countries had a great rapport and military alliance when times warranted.

"Cooper?" Shadow called and stopped. Cooper's shoulders hunched. Guilt? He searched the surrounding area, although he'd been doing just that since he'd seen his team. But there was no sign of her. He'd left Arianna inside the store. Maybe she was still in there. Or better yet getting medical attention. He twisted looking but couldn't see her.

"Cooper," he repeated in an ominous tone of voice, hating he was immediately thinking the worst. Surely she hadn't been killed. He'd left her alive and well in the store. But he hadn't actually checked her over to see if a stray bullet had caught her. "Where is she?"

Cooper took a deep breath but it was Mason who answered.

"She was airlifted out a half hour ago."

Shadow locked down inside. She was gone. He hadn't been able to say good-bye. There'd been no time. No one had let him know. He'd been busy helping the old lady and Arianna had been shipped out alone.

God, she'd have been a wreck. And he hadn't been there for her. Of course he hadn't. He'd done his job. Done what he was supposed to do. Damn it.

Mason, his gaze steady on his face while none of the others would look at him, said in a low voice, "She's at the hospital."

He nodded. "Good, that leg needs attention." He was damn proud of himself for keeping his voice steady. Inside though, he was shattering. And couldn't afford to let anyone know. He blinked and stared across the way, lost. The world of his, darkening. Shadows filling up the places she'd opened up, letting in the sunlight. Now the light was gone.

Foolish.

Cheesy.

Stupid.

But it was the way he felt.

Cooper spoke up. "She didn't want to go, but she didn't have a choice. Like you said, her leg needed attention." He raised his gaze to Shadow's dark hooded one. "I told her we'd go to the hospital to see her if we could. I promised her that she'd see us again."

And the shadows moved to the other side, letting the light shine once again.

"Good. That's important to her." Shadow turned and walked toward the store. Needing to leave. To get away. To be alone. Before the others understood just how much she meant to him. And how much her needing that promise did for his soul. It didn't matter that she'd made Cooper promise. It had been intended for him.

"We'll be leaving in ten minutes," Mason called. "We're hours from the hospital."

"I'll be ready," he said in a controlled voice. "Just want to make sure of something."

The men watched him as he strode inside. He could feel their scrutiny burning into his back. Once in the store, a quick glance confirming he was alone, he walked to the end where she'd been crouched the last time he'd seen her, and for just a moment he let down his guard, and whispered, "Thank God. Ten minutes. We're coming sweetheart. We'll be there soon."

CHAPTER 19

WAKING IN THE hospital sucked. Sure she was comfortable and she was feeling better and not being cramped in a back seat with her legs stretched out across the guys' knees but she was…alone.

Was there anything worse? She wasn't sure how she was going to be able to go back to her condo and her teaching job. She currently taught at a private girls' school. How bloody predictable was that? She loved her kids, but had thought often that she'd like to work with those less fortunate. Her father would have a heart attack if he knew what she was thinking.

Then again, her poor father wasn't going to be able to react to anything anymore. Even if he survived this, he wasn't going to be around for too much longer.

She'd love to teach the not so privileged kids. She wasn't sure she had the temperament for inner city kids, there was definitely a skill needed for them that she didn't think she had. The public system interested her though. Everyone seemed to think private school would mean she could avoid most of the problems prevalent in the public system. But she'd found growing up that the private school system had just as many problems. There were still drugs, booze, and sex at the younger ages. Cheating was rampant and the class eliteness was horrific.

Yet she'd followed the same path for teaching. Now she realized it wasn't enough. It kept her in her comfort zone when there was so much else available. She needed more. And if her mind suggested she explore opportunities in the direction of San Diego and a very large well known base there, well who could blame her?

Her stomach growled. She couldn't remember when she'd last eaten. The doctor's had given her a shot of something in her IV like vitamins or something, but she wished for food. Like a real meal. She'd missed lunch as it had been served while she'd been in the ER. Now she'd have to wait for dinner and her stomach was already weighing the odds between the value of a hospital lunch versus no food, and she realized it didn't matter how bad it was, she'd be happy to have anything. She yawned and snuggled under the covers again. She was still so damn tired. She dozed peacefully just under the surface. When she heard the louder footsteps on the hallways she figured it was the doctors on their rounds.

But there was something odd in the air. She opened her eyes. And smiled.

She didn't turn. She didn't trust her heart. It was doing the happy dance inside her chest. She knew exactly who was at the doorway. She said slowly in a low voice, without turning to look at him, "Hello, Shadow."

She sensed his surprise. He walked into the room a few steps. "May I come in?"

She rolled over, saw he was alone and beamed up at him. She opened her arms and was gratified to see him reach out for her. She hugged him closer. God she'd missed this. Him.

When she could trust her voice, she cried, "I hated to leave you without saying good-bye."

"It's what had to be done. Your leg needed care." He looked down at her sheet covered limbs and asked, "How is it?"

"It's great," she exclaimed. "The doctor said you guys did a wonderful job."

"Of course," he said casually. "Our medical training for field dressings is pretty extensive."

"Then why did I have to come here," she said, feeling aggravated at knowing she could have stayed with him.

He placed a finger against her lips. "In case there was more damage than we could see."

She kissed his finger and he smiled down at her. Such a warm caring smile, she sighed happily. "Are you okay? I know it got pretty hairy for a while there."

"It did. Everything is being mopped up now. We weren't needed at this stage so we're on our way home."

Her face fell. "Without me?"

"You are staying here until they can arrange for you to go home."

"On a commercial flight?" She hated the sound of that. "Can I go home with you? Surely I need to go in for debriefing. I'm a US citizen and the recovered victim of a kidnapping. The senator's daughter. Are you sure I can't come home with you?" she said in a wheedling voice.

"We could be going home on a commercial flight too," he said. "No idea what the plans are for the moment."

"Perfect. Let me come with you. Then at least if I am too tired or injured I can trust that you'll make sure I get home."

"Which is another good reason why you are staying here," he said.

Her face fell. For a moment there she'd so hoped.

"You aren't ready to fly yet," he added in a soothing voice.

"Sure I am," she said stoutly. "If I was ready for everything else that happened over the last few days, flying home with you guys is hardly an issue."

A voice from the doorway called out. They turned to stare as Swede carrying two large bags of something that smelled heavenly and the rest of the gang carrying coffee arrived. The last man in was Cooper, and he arrived a few seconds later, carrying a huge bouquet of flowers in his arms.

She cried out and reached for them.

"They are gorgeous."

"And they are from all of us," Cooper said. "Even the silent dude here. He just wouldn't wait for us to arrive together. He raced ahead."

She lay the flowers on her lap. "Thank you." And she reached up to hug him, then Swede, Hawk, Dane and finally Mason.

They all stepped back, grinning. She was so damn happy. "I missed you guys. I hated leaving without you all."

"Hey, it broke my heart to put you on that helicopter," Cooper admitted. "I knew Shadow here would shoot me for it too."

"He didn't though, did he?" She searched Cooper's face, saw the grin then caught Shadow rolling his eyes. "Of course you wouldn't shoot him, but that doesn't mean you wouldn't have smacked him around some."

"Not likely, he's bigger than me," Shadow said with a straight face.

The others snickered.

"That's only because he had to do so much physical therapy after getting injured," she explained. "I'm sure if you worked out, you'd get that size too."

The others laughed.

"I was kidding," Shadow said, shaking his head.

She sighed. "Right, of course you were." She winced. "Speaking of which, the doctor wants me to see a shrink. Please let me go home with you guys. I really don't want to have to speak to anyone about what happened."

"Actually, I'm not sure that you should be speaking to anyone yet." Shadow turned to Mason. "It will involve her relationship with her father and family and the events leading up to this. As what that is isn't exactly clear at this point, should she be talking about any of this to someone without clearance?"

Mason pursed his lips. "A good point. But not sure it's enough to stop you from talking to a trauma counselor. You might need to do that at some point."

"Maybe, but at home would be better. Besides," she glanced over at Cooper, "I was telling Cooper some of the dirty family history."

"And I didn't fill you in on what the one kidnapper said, about this being a double job," Shadow interrupted her. "You and your father weren't supposed to survive."

She stared at him. "Just me and my father? Not all of us?"

"According to the kidnapper, you and your father weren't supposed to make it out alive. When we rescued you, it changed things."

"And I was explaining to Cooper that I believe if my father dies then his estate would go to my stepmother and if something happened to her then to my brother. And that means his guardian would have control."

"And who is that guardian?"

She sighed. "My father's aide. Who is also my step-uncle. My stepmother's brother. He's the one who made the arrangements for our trip."

The men gave several exclamations as they worked out the angles on the kidnapping and who could be responsible.

Shadow reached over and grabbed her hand. "We'll get to the bottom of this."

"I know you will." She reached up to stroke his face. "I just hate the thought that even though I'll be home in a few days, this nightmare might not be over. I really need it to be over."

"It will be," Swede said from the side. He moved a small swing table across her lap. "But before any of this can be over, we need food. So let's take a look at what we've got."

"I'm so hungry. That chocolate bar was a long time ago."

"Did you get anything since?" Swede asked her in shock. "Hell, you're skinny enough without losing more meals." He opened the takeout bag and proceeded to unload enough food for a dozen people. Or maybe a half dozen SEALs.

SHADOW HADN'T REALIZED how acceptance, approval, had such an impact on someone. Arianna blossomed with the men. They were all friendly and joking, gently teasing, but he knew the atmosphere, their actions for what it was. They all approved. Of her. For him.

How sappy. But it made him feel great. She was something. Not unlike the other women the men had paired up with. And yet, different. She was herself. Was he being foolish thinking that maybe they could try for a relationship? He didn't have anything good to say about the highbrow females he'd met in the past, and Arianna was definitely one of them.

But she was also herself. And very down to earth.

She had a lot of processing to do now though and not the least was the death of her father. He had died, but had she been told? Everyone had tried to prepare her and she understood he'd had little chance of surviving, but that wasn't the same thing as hearing the definitive statement. He'd noticed that no one had brought it up, including Arianna herself. As if she knew but couldn't stand to have the truth voiced because then she'd be forced to deal with the emotional onslaught of grief.

And who was he to judge her for that? He locked everything inside. She let it all pour out. In public...that wasn't much fun. She'd try to wait for a private time to release all that pain.

That her own family might have had a hand in this nightmare was not hard to believe. He'd seen too much of the world to be surprised any more. Not to mention there was the stepmom in there too. If she lived through the trauma then she was the one who inherited it all. And that made their current theory implausible. But she'd still have to be careful. As in more than careful. At least until this mess was over.

With a full plate in his hand, he glanced around at the hospital room and smiled. His brothers in arms were men he could trust with anyone, but especially with Arianna. They'd bend over backwards to make her happy as Shadow had done for each of their partners.

Content, he picked up his fork. And stared at what was on the end of it. He was a meat and potatoes guy. Most of the men were. But this time they'd let Swede shop. And that was always a mistake. That man could eat. Like seriously eat. And never had a problem trying new foods. Often bought meals the guys didn't recognize. And while all SEALs ate healthy, Swede started at one end and ate his way through to the other end of his plate then started working on anything else close by. So Shadow had to make up his mind quickly if he wanted second servings – or it would be too late.

While the others wrangled gently there was a hard knock on the door and an older lady walked in.

"Excuse me. Are you supposed to be here?" she asked in a voice laced with the potential to breathe fire on their heads if they gave the wrong answer.

Shadow had had a teacher like her in school. With just one look you were cringing in your shoes.

They had the right to be here – sometime. He just didn't know when and from the look on Arianna's face, she didn't want them to go anywhere anytime soon.

Shadow stood and straightened his shoulders, and in a low lethal level voice, he said, "Yes, and do you?"

She glared at him, but he refused to back down. Arianna had been through enough, and if she needed him to defend her from one more assault then he was prepared to do so.

"I'm the trauma counselor," she snapped, her nose in the air and not backing down either. "I need to speak with her, assess her state of mind."

No one could miss Arianna's squeak of horror.

"I'm fine," she rushed to say. "These men are the ones who rescued me."

"That might be but after the trauma you've been through the last thing you need is a reminder of those events by having the same men surround you. They need to disappear and now." She waved her hand at them.

"No, you don't understand," Arianna said, her voice slightly stronger. "I feel better with them around."

"No. And no, and no. You don't. You are looking at these soldiers in the wrong light. They are not your friends. They were doing a job. It's over. Now your job is to heal and move past these events. You can't look at these men as your personal heroes forever."

Shadow opened his mouth to blast her.

Mason spun and glared at her.

Swede slowly straightened to his full height.

And not one of them got a chance to say anything as Arianna's voice cut through the tension into his room.

"I'm sorry, you appear to have been given the wrong information. I don't need trauma counseling. I'm fine. Also, I don't need to forget that these are my friends because you are wrong, they are my friends, and I'm proud to call them friend in return." Her voice rose as she fired the next volley at the woman standing frozen. "And don't you ever... And I mean ever insult these heroes in such a way again. They are heroes. To me. And my country."

Arianna's chest heaved as she now stood at the side of her bed, and taking several hobbling steps, stood in front of Shadow. "No one insults my friends while I am still standing. So take that attitude and your counseling skills back out that door. You are not wanted here."

And if that wasn't going to get the job done, Shadow had no idea what it would take. The poor woman almost ran from the room.

Shadow grinned down at the injured sprite who'd taken on the dragon lady to defend her warriors. She'd love that imagery. And he was such a sap. He put down his plate of food, snagged her up in his arms and laid her back down in the bed. He kissed her hard.

When she opened her mouth to snap at him, he popped the mystery meat into her mouth.

"Chew on that and not on me."

She chewed but still glared. He added for all the men to hear, "And thanks for the defense, sweetheart. But you didn't have to. We have thick skins."

"You might, but I don't when it comes to others. So remember that." She narrowed her gaze and finally managed to swallow. "No one insults you while I'm here. Got that?"

Hiding grins of their own, they all nodded obediently. And Shadow realized something else. He was really hooked. He sat back down and picked up his plate and proceeded to eat, waiting for her to calm down. But he knew she'd be the talk of the trip home now. She'd defended all of them. Stood up and blasted back at some poor woman who'd insulted them.

Except the men had been okay with the insult. They'd heard worse. Arianna had been the one to take umbrage. Protective. Caring. The same as she was with her brother.

There was a commotion outside and they all looked at each other. Now came the big guns.

Instead it was the doctor. He walked in and smiled. "You are the heroes, I presume."

They all nodded, sheepish grins on their faces.

"Nice to meet you," the doctor said in an amiable, let's–all–get–along voice. "Now we do have a problem though. I'd suggested Miss Stephenson take some time to work with the trauma counselor—"

"And your advice was taken into consideration, and I've decided to refuse it," Arianna said coolly from her bed. "I do understand that I'll need to speak with someone. I'm sure my doctor at home has someone he can recommend."

The doctor studied her for a long moment then nodded. "As long as you do, my dear. It's important to keep it all in perspective so you can move forward with your life."

"No problem," she said, beaming at him. "I'm feeling wonderful."

"And you do look much better." He smiled. "So maybe reconnecting with your friends is the first step."

She nodded. "Thanks for caring."

He motioned to the plates of food. "I gather you won't be needing dinner either?" he asked in a dry voice. "You appear to have enough here for the entire hospital."

"Just Swede," she said with a straight face, pointing to Swede. "He's a hard man to fill." Swede once again stood up and dwarfed the doctor who laughed and shook his head.

"Sounds like you're in good hands." With a smile, he added, "I'll take my leave."

Mason hopped to his feet and handed his empty plate to Cooper. "If I could have a word with you, Doctor..."

Surprised, the doctor who already stood in the open doorway, said, "Of course."

Mason stepped outside the room and the door was shut, leaving the rest of them to stare and wonder at what Mason was up too.

Shadow hoped he knew, but knowing Mason as he did...it

could be anything.

Still he caught Arianna biting her bottom lip in worry as she stared at the closed door. "Sunshine and rainbows, remember?"

With a confused look, she stared at him. Then a slow understanding dawned in her eyes. "Right. And don't forget the unicorns."

He laughed. The others looked at the two of them in confusion then shook their heads.

Shadow studied the containers of food stacked beside Swede and asked, "Any leftovers?"

"Nope." But Swede's grin was a mile wide.

"You couldn't have eaten all that already? Aren't you on a diet?"

At Swede's look of horror the others burst out laughing. Hawk reached for the closest stack of containers and passed them to Shadow. "Help yourself. You know he'll finish all of it no matter how much there is, so get yours first."

On that note, Shadow refilled Arianna's and his plates. Then handed the leftovers back to the big man who stared at the almost empty container like a puppy who hadn't eaten in days.

"You can have mine," Arianna offered with a big smile, handing her plate to Swede.

He gently pushed it back. "No way. You need to eat. There's more."

Happy and content for the first time in his memory, Shadow watched the rest of his team wrangle in fun over the food.

CHAPTER 20

THEY WERE ALL little boys. Arianna watched the fun and games as the men ploughed through what was left to eat. Mason still hadn't come back. It was worrisome. Was it about her? What else could it be about? It wasn't like Mason knew the doctor. Then again, maybe he had medical questions. She couldn't second-guess this one.

When the door opened up to let Mason back in, they all stopped and waited.

"And…" Hawk asked. "What's the latest?"

"We're flying commercial all the way. If we can switch out in Seattle to a military flight then we will."

"Good stuff." Dane stood up and collected the dirty paper dishes in a big stack. He quickly bagged the empty containers next. "When?"

"Flight leaves in three hours. We need to return the truck at the airport."

Cooper hopped to his feet. "That means leaving now."

"Pretty much. We have just one more thing to do."

Arianna's heart sank. Her stomach wanted to revolt. In fact, she wanted to curl up alone under the covers and cry. Time for that in a little bit apparently. They'd be gone in minutes. Damn. She'd been hoping.

"What else is there to do?" Hawk asked impatiently when Mason didn't answer.

She glanced over at Mason, realizing they were all looking at him for that answer. She studied the twinkle in his eyes. And hope surged inside. "Me? Are you waiting for me?"

He nodded. "The doctor is going to put a thicker bandage on that leg so you can travel easier and the agreement is you're to check in at a clinic tomorrow morning. If you agree to those terms, you can fly home with us."

"Yes," she shouted. "Yes."

The men grinned.

"Good. In that case, I suggest we clear out so the doctor can do his thing. Then we have a plane to catch."

"Thank you. Thank you. *Thank you,*" she chanted as the men gathered up their coats and slowly walked out to wait in the hallway.

Shadow was the last to leave. She beamed up at him. Then her face fell. "Mason won't get in trouble, will he?"

"No. You were right earlier. All those reasons are valid for bringing you home with us. You are going to have to speak with the investigators when you get there though."

She nodded. "I know. That's no problem. I'd have to explain to someone. Several someone's most likely. You guys killed everyone else…"

"Not the one man. We never saw him again."

Right. That brought her up short. "Not a good reminder."

"No, but something we have to keep in mind."

The doctor walked in just then. Shadow leaned over and kissed her. "I'll wait outside."

And he left too.

The doctor smiled at her. "So that's the way of it."

She nodded. "I sure hope it is."

He laughed, pulled the sheet back and said, "Now let's take a look."

And take a look he did. After the check–up, he quickly bound her leg. "I'm not sure if your pants are here…"

"They should be around," she said, hating to think she might not be able to leave because she didn't have clothes. "I was actually wearing a spare pair of pants from one of the men."

He nodded. "I'll send one of the nurses in with your belongings."

He disappeared and a nurse reappeared with a paper bag and her pack. "Here's what we had for you."

Arianna opened the paper bag and pulled out the same black pants she'd been wearing. She had her spare jeans in her pack but the reasons for wearing Shadow's pants still held. She'd thought they were sweatpants but instead now that she had a chance to examine them she could see they were an underlay for the cold. No wonder she'd never felt the chill in the air when she'd been outside. These things were wonderful. With the nurse's help, she dressed in the same pants but with a clean shirt and her vest she had in the pack. She wished she had managed a shower but given the choices she'd forgo that for a ride home. She'd be able to sleep in her own bed tonight. And could shower in her own shower. Just the sound of that made her grin.

That was so worth being dirty for a little while longer. By the time she was dressed, her hair brushed and twisted into a knot and secured at the back of her head and her pack slung over her shoulder, she took a last look around the small room and gave a happy sigh. She was going home.

Picking up her bouquet of flowers and with a big grin, she walked out to the hallway and her new friends.

Cooper said, "You look great."

She beamed. "I feel great. Dressed again, a full tummy and now on my way home. Yay me."

They laughed and said, "Paperwork then we're on our way."

The paperwork was just a few signatures then they led her, using crutches Shadow had found for her, outside to the truck.

IT BOTHERED SHADOW that there were doubts about who was behind the kidnapping. Could the kidnapper he'd talked to been serious? He'd sounded it. But that meant that someone who wanted the senator and his daughter dead, got wind of the kidnapping and might have made their own deal. Was that possible? Sure, but how *probable* was it? There were a lot of assholes out there but most people went through their entire life never brushing up against the seriously bad ones.

He could see setting it up so that the kidnapping was intended to go wrong and have the two – or more die. But never Kevin. If the entire family was wiped out, the money would not go to the right person. That was key. And narrowed the field.

The investigators needed to check out the senator's aide. And anyone else close enough to know the details of the will. Like the lawyers and the witnesses to the will. Not to mention, did anyone know who those people were?

"Arianna, have you seen your father's will?"

She shook her head. Not even the return to an unpleasant subject seemed to dull her good humor. She'd been smiling nonstop since they boarded the flight. The first one was taking them into Seattle direct, and they'd be home a second flight later. But he wouldn't be leaving her alone until she was safe and tucked up in her own bed.

"No. I haven't and he's never spoken to me about it." Pulling her attention from the window she turned to look at him. "Why?"

"Just wondering how many people know the details."

She wrinkled up her face. "No idea. No one has ever contacted me."

"And…" he hated to ask this, as it made him sound crass, "If you die, who does your estate go to?"

"Kevin," she said promptly. "There are other family members around but I don't know them. If I die then he's the one who needs the money the most."

Mason, sitting across from them, asked, "Can you give us a list of anyone in your family who might be in line to inherit?"

"Sure."

Shadow handed her a small pad of paper and a pen. She stared at the blank page for a long moment as if collecting her thoughts. Then the names showed up. Two then a third. She drew a line underneath and started writing other names down.

"I think we should look at the stepmom," Swede said from beside Mason. "It's usually someone who will inherit and she's the surviving spouse and will have her son's money to look after."

Dane agreed. He leaned across the aisle adding, "She didn't want to go supposedly, so just the right amount of reluctance. She was hurt but not badly. Her son was never hurt, which is what she'd want, and she gets rid of an aging domineering husband leaving her in the honey seat."

Shadow had to agree that in theory the stepmother was a

good suspect. But did she have the stomach for killing her husband. Then again, she hadn't killed him, someone else had. And having a killer was a different story.

"What if the kidnappers contacted someone in the Senate, asking for ransom? And that person took advantage of the moment and turned the deal into something else," Shadow said slowly. "The only reason *we* knew who was involved was Arianna's photo sent to her father's aide."

"Which should in theory clear him of being a participant."

"Unless he knew how to contact the kidnappers and then made a deal for himself. Although, with the senator and Arianna dead, the money goes to the stepmother and the boy, and not him." Mason paused then shrugged. "Unless he can move up in his career from this somehow."

"But why Arianna?"

Everyone turned to look at her. She shrugged. "I have money from my mother's side of the family, but it's not much comparatively."

The others winced, a few sent side long glances at Shadow who slouched lower in his chair at the news.

"Your idea of not much isn't necessarily everyone's," he muttered. Of course she had money. Probably tons of the shit. Like why would he fall for a rich woman when someone who lived at the poverty line would suit him as well? He wasn't into glitz and glamour. Sideways, he took his first look at her clothing. Decent t–shirt, nice warm vest, probably expensive. Her pack had been a popular outdoor brand. A good brand for everyday outdoor people. They carried a die hard line that was hard-wearing and durable. Hers wasn't that level. Yet she wasn't carrying a glamor girl pretty version. So there was hope for her yet. Then he caught sight of her pants. And he barely held back his grin. She was wearing *his* pants still. And not only wearing. She rocked the look.

So what if she had money. She looked damn good in his underwear.

CHAPTER 21

FOR ALL HER initial exuberance at finally being on the way home, it was waning quickly. There was also a sense of melancholy. Arianna had been devastated at not saying good-bye to the men before, but now there were going to be plenty ahead of her. More pain. More loss. More to deal with.

She yawned. They'd boarded the second flight. This time a military flight as Mason had managed to pull his magic and get them onto one. They'd connected up with Markus and Evan at the same time. This type of flight didn't offer the same frills or extras but was more comforting to her own way of thinking. She leaned her head against Shadow's shoulder and closed her eyes. "Wake me when we land," she murmured, knowing that he had little choice but to do so.

Even though exhausted, she couldn't sleep. She drifted in and out, hearing the men talk. Bits and pieces of disjointed conversations all in a low monotone. She had hours of flying yet and needed to rest, but her own mind was caught on the problems. Anything to avoid looking at what her life would be like in a few hours. Alone.

She shifted restlessly.

"You're not sleeping," Shadow murmured for her ears only. "Leg bothering you?"

"No," she whispered. "Just life bothering me."

He reached across for her hand and grasped it gently in his. "It will work out. Stay positive."

With a grin, she answered, "Really? Is that you saying that to me?"

A deep chuckle rolled out from his mouth. He was so damn sexy.

"Maybe some of that happy-go-lucky attitude is rubbing off on me."

"Oh dear. Your friends won't recognize you." She'd love to think some of her normally positive happy outlook on life was brightening up his world too. He was a sweetheart, but so didn't believe in all the things she wanted for her world. They were darkness and light.

"I guess we're opposites, aren't we?" she asked in a small voice. Was that a good thing or bad?

"In some ways. But in many no, we're the same."

"Almost home." She yawned again. "I should go to the hospital. See my stepmother." She paused. Then added, "And say good-bye to my father." She'd stomped on that inevitability until later. When she could deal with it.

He gathered her hand. "Your stepmother, she's not there. She's at home resting." He lowered his voice, and said, "And your dad…well, you can do that tomorrow."

Her breath caught in the back of her throat. She shifted so she could look in his eyes. She didn't have to ask, she could see it. Shadow shook his head. She bit her lip and let him tug her into his arms where he just held her. She already knew inside, yet getting that confirmation, well, that hurt. "He'd appreciate going out in battle. A martyr for his beliefs," she said in low tones.

He nodded. "Kevin is lucky to have you," he whispered.

"Not really." Arianna looked at him. "I should have called him before this."

"You haven't had time to do anything, especially to think about others. He's been told you're fine. That's the important part."

She offered a wan smile, determined to hold the tears back. There would be time to grieve later. In private where she could honor him the way he'd like to be remembered. She had to get home first. She stuffed the emotions deep inside until later. "Right. The rest is just time to heal and reconnect." She frowned thinking about all the suppositions they'd thrown out earlier. "Has someone warned my stepmother that she might be next in line to die?"

Shadow looked down at her. "No idea. Besides, whoever is behind this had a great way to get rid of her already. They let her live. There must be a reason."

"Right. More conspiracy theories. Hate them." She looked down at the lights below. It was late and the city was lit up like a beautiful Christmas tree of lights. She might not like all the nasty theories, but it didn't change the fact that because of what the one killer said, her world was even more unstable than before. And now her father had died. She knew it, understood it, accepted it and knew she wasn't even close to dealing with it. The tears rose. Ruthlessly. She shoved them back down until later.

She had to get through this next couple of hours. Then they'd be gone and she could deal with the loss. So many losses.

"What time is it?"

"It's almost eleven."

First she had to get from the airport home. She froze. She was in a military plane heading for a military airport. That meant outside San Diego most likely. The naval base where the team was from. She wasn't home yet. Newport Beach was at least an hour away. Likely two. And she had no idea how to get from the one to the other. Shit.

The plane landed with so little ceremony and custom hassles she wished she could fly this way all the time. There were quick good-bye hugs from the men and then there was just Shadow standing beside her.

Forlornly she stared at the men's retreating backs. "I'm going to miss them."

"You'll see them again."

She laughed. "I hope not if it means getting kidnapped again."

"It won't. Come on." He led her back outside to a large parking lot and a black Jeep. He unlocked it, threw the two bags into the back. "Get in."

Grinning, she hopped in. "Nice Jeep."

"Ha. Several of us own them." He turned it on and reversed out of the parking spot. "Now let's get you the last leg to your home."

HE'D SEEN HER worry over how she'd get home. He was hardly going to dump her at the airport. She was injured. He'd considered taking her to his place for the night and driving her home in the morning, but what she'd been through, he thought she'd rest best in her own bed.

She leaned back and closed her eyes.

He put on low peaceful music and drove down the highway. He was due some shut eye himself. But not yet. She came first.

At the outskirts to Newport Beach he brought up her address on his phone. She wasn't far from where he was idling on the curb. She slept gently. He'd have to wake her soon for the house keys. He hoped after all she'd been through she still had them. He pulled up in front of a small brownstone complex with wide lazy porches in the front. Nice.

"Arianna. Is this home?"

She murmured something unintelligible and opened her eyes. When she saw the building beside her, she cried out in joy. "Oh my God. I'm home."

And he realized he'd done the right thing bringing her here. He got out and grabbed her bag from the back then brought her crutches to her. On the sidewalk she looked up and beamed.

"You know how many times I figured I'd never see this place again?"

"Just goes to show you that life is full of surprises." He led her to the stairway then scooped her up, crutches and all and carried her to the porch level. "Have your keys?"

"I do." She rummaged around in her pack and triumphantly pulled out a set.

He took them from her and opened the door. And paused to let her go inside. She hobbled forward, her happy sigh making him smile. "I'm so damn glad to be here," she whispered. She stared at the stairs in front of her. "But doing those stairs with my leg is going to be a bitch."

He laughed and shut the door behind her. Turning, he swept her off her feet again and carried her to the second floor. And her bedroom. She flicked the light switch on flowing the soft colored room with warm light. "Oh my God. Even better, my bed."

Still grinning, he laid her down on the covers. She immediately bounced to her feet and threw her arms around his neck and kissed him. "Thank you for seeing I made it home."

"I told you I would." Hating to leave but knowing it was time, and he had a long drive home, he hugged her close then stepped back. "Now get some rest."

And he walked to the door.

He glanced back to see her fighting to hold back tears. "Hey, it's going to be okay."

She shook her head. "If you walk out that door it won't ever be okay."

He froze. He wanted to stay. Of course he did. Any man would. And it would certainly be his desired next step but what about…her reasoning…

"This can't be just so you don't have to say good-bye."

She shook her head. "It's not," but her voice was low, soft.

He narrowed his gaze at her. He'd only stay for the right reasons.

In a low but more confident voice, she said, "Just stay the night, then. You don't want that long drive back right now. Sleep. Rest."

So had he misjudged what she was asking? Damn he hated this.

He was no good at pussy footing around the issue. Better to know now. "If I stay it won't be to sleep on the couch downstairs."

And her smile was breathtaking. "Then you'd better sleep here." She stood up slowly and in spite of her best attempts to not show it, winced. And he knew he shouldn't leave her alone to fend for herself tonight at all. She motioned at the bed. "With me."

"Come on. You're in no shape for anything right now."

She shot him a look. "Really? How do you feel about taking a shower with me?"

And that smile of hers set him on fire. He shouldn't. She was hurt. But damn he wanted to.

She hobbled to the bathroom, her shirt tugged over her shoulder and tossed on the floor beside him. He hesitated.

"I haven't had a shower in days and I'm covered in blood." Her bra was tossed outside to land in the middle of the floor. He swallowed hard. Oh shit. There was only so much resistance he could put into place here, and knowing it wasn't in her best interest was fast waning as an excuse. When his pants and yes her panties were flung out the door, followed by two small socks, he couldn't think of anything else but her standing with that damn bandage in the shower. Alone.

When the water turned on he knew he was lost.

He stripped off his clothes and left them in a pile beside hers. And walked into the bathroom, already heavily aroused. Blood pounded through his body. He needed her. Like now.

Calm down, Shadow. She needed a careful lover not a fast, take her hard against the shower wall, type of lover. He stood outside the frosted glass doors and watched the water sluice down her slender from. He closed his eyes, willing his body to slow down, reaching for the last bit of control.

"Are you going to join me or just watch?"

And she opened the door inviting him in.

CHAPTER 22

S HE HADN'T WANTED him to leave. It was one of those moments where she knew that if she didn't say what was needed to be said then she'd regret it for the rest of her life. She wanted Shadow forever. If she only got one night then she only got one night. It was more than she was going to have if she didn't tell him how she felt. Even then it felt stilted, awkward. Partly because he didn't come rushing over to take her into his arms. Followed by her own realization of how dirty she was. And then she understood what she needed to do.

Now seeing him standing on the other side of the glass watching her... Oh God. She could be standing in ice water right now and she wouldn't notice. She needed him and now. She knew her leg was an issue. But she knew they'd find a way. And if she had a little pain to go with the joy, then that was all right too.

He stepped inside the large shower and picked up the bottle of shampoo. She couldn't see him clearly through the water in her eyes but when he turned her so he could shampoo her long hair, she could feel him hard and ready, nudging her hip. When his fingers slid through her locks and then dug in lightly to her scalp, she moaned.

"Feels so good," she whispered.

And he massaged her scalp a little more. When he turned her to face him, she leaned her forehead against his chest and accepted the ministrations. She loved the careful way he worked shampoo through her hair. When his fingers worked down to her neck and shoulder muscles she groaned and looped her arms around his back to snuggle up close. Her breasts pressed against his chest, his erection nestled against her belly.

She didn't want the moment to end. When those wonderful fingers slid down her spine carefully massaging the bank of muscles on either side, she whimpered in joy.

"How can I be so sore?" she asked. "I didn't do anything."

"Running and twisting, climbing trees, sitting in the truck for hours in a position not conducive to relaxing and then there were the hours in the store…"

"Well, if you're going to put it that way," she muttered with a small laugh, "I guess all of me is going to be sore."

His hands slid down to her hips and dug deep, working the muscles inside. She melted. When they slipped lower to cup her cheeks and pull her up against him, she shivered.

"Feels so good," she said.

"You feel good," he whispered against her ear, and the heat of his voice sent tingles down her spine. Then he kissed her ear, gently tracing the outside skin with his tongue and dropping kisses behind and below, his mouth tracing down her long neck to the curve of her shoulders. Her arms slipped up his hot wet chest, her fingers sliding into his thick hair. She clung to him as he retraced his steps, dropping kisses on to her chin and over to her mouth. He'd kissed her several times already but when he took her mouth this time it was like nothing she'd experienced ever before. It was heart stoppingly beautiful. And she couldn't get enough. When he withdrew his head she followed. She needed more. So much more. He kissed her again, tiny gentle kisses across her eyes and temple, all the while hugging her close.

So tender. So caring. So loving. She could feel his restraint, felt the shudders of thinly held control work their way down his strong body. He was afraid of hurting her. And she couldn't have cared less. After what she'd been through this...his touch...being here with him...heaven.

"Love me, Shadow, please love me..."

He slid his hand into her hair and tugged her head back. Something had shifted. This time when he took her mouth it was deep and dark and possessive. His other hand slid up her sleek wet body to cup her breast. She cried out, but he inhaled the sound looking for more. She whimpered as he squeezed gently, his finger rubbing the nipple, waking her body. She slid her hand between their bodies and found him. Hot. Hard. Ready. And she squeezed his length, her fingers sliding down then back up as she explored the size of him.

His groan was heaven to her ears. She slid her hand back down to cup the sacs below, he gasped and pulled her hand away.

"Too much."

"Not enough."

He gave a half groan. "Impatient."

"With you...yes."

His free hand slid down to cup her left cheek, in one scoop he bent, lifted her thigh over his arm and raised her high and using his body, pinned her in place against the tiled back of the shower. She gasped as he nudged up against her center. She wrapped her legs around his waist. So close. And so damn far away.

"Are you sure?"

She groaned in laughter. "Never more so."

But still he hesitated.

She dropped tiny kisses on his chin, his neck, her hands frantic on his back and arms. "I'm protected, if that's the concern."

A shudder rippled across his body. "It wasn't but it should have been," he said in a midnight dark voice. "You make me forget everything."

"Good," she said rubbing her breasts slowly from side to side against his chest. "It's only a fraction of what you do to me. And yet, it's not enough."

He kissed her again, his other hand sliding up and down, teasing, tantalizing, stroking her to a fevered pitch and just when she didn't think she could stand it anymore, he slid his hand down, grabbed her hip.

And entered her on a deep surge.

And stilled.

She gasped in shock and in joy, wanting to weep as emotions poured through her.

"Did I hurt you?" he muttered, his body shuddering in place.

"No, never," she cried. "But if you don't move, I'm going to hurt you."

And with a deep chuckle, he plunged again and again. Pinned against the wall, her feet not even on the floor, she was slammed by his passion, her need rising but her response stymied because she couldn't move. She was completely helpless. Left to his mercy. And his timing.

And Lord, he was good. Just when she didn't think she'd reach that peak, so damn close and so frustratingly far away, he bent and took one nipple deep into mouth and suckled hard.

The pulsations started deep inside and worked outward in ever increasing waves as the climax rolled through her. She cried out, her body lay in a state of wonder as he pounded and pounded and…ground against her, his own groan melding with hers as he found his own release.

She rested her head against her chest and grinned happily. When she could trust her voice, she said, "I always knew SEALs were good in the water."

He gave a great shout of laugher, wrapped her in his arms and pushing open the shower, he reached for the towel hanging beside the door and wrapped it around her back. Then, he carefully carried her to her bed and slowly lowered her down.

"Now sleep. I'm not going anywhere."

She reached up and kissed him, lovingly, pouring all the emotions that were overwhelming her and bringing tears to her eyes. "I don't want you to go anywhere ever again."

And she slept.

HE WATCHED HER crash, physically and mentally, emotionally. As if overload had happened and it had been too much. She literally closed her eyes and was out. He slowly withdrew and stood up. With the towel he dried her off. And wondered at the leg. Leave it wet? Dry it? Change it? Deciding that leaving it as is for the moment was likely to cause the least amount of damage in the long run, he gently tugged the bedding out from under her and covered her back up. He returned to the shower and cleaned up the bathroom floor as much as he could. They'd tracked a lot of water on the way to the bed and he didn't want her to slip and fall if she needed to go to the washroom in the night. She murmured in her sleep. He returned to her side and stood for a moment watching her. She shifted uneasily. He reached down and placed a hand on her temple. "Easy, sweetie, you're safe now."

Instantly, she stilled and fell into a deeper sleep.

He stared around the small room and wondered why he couldn't sleep. His instincts wouldn't shut down. He was tired. Could use a power nap but with no one to watch her back while he was out, he couldn't do it.

Something was wrong and he didn't know what. He grabbed up his phone and wandered the bedroom, his fingers searching for information that would shed light on this mess. He also sent a couple of texts. Had he spent too much of his lifetime looking for bad guys and competent ones at that...that the idiot bad guys seemed to be just too simple. Still, he had nothing to go on. But he hadn't been kidding when he'd said the reasons for doing this was going to boil down to sex, power, or money. And sometimes all three.

There was an odd looking couch bench chair thing at the window, he sat down and studied the information coming in. Everyone knew they'd planned to return this night. So the senator's office could know as well. If nothing else, Kevin had been told and he'd likely told several other people. How could he not? He was eight. And this was his adored sister.

But that didn't mean something nasty wasn't planned for Arianna's return. Especially if she stood between a killer and his prize.

With messages coming and going, he hated the warning sensation at the nape of his neck. Yet he couldn't seem to get the idea out of his head. If he was on the killing streak and she was on his list then he'd have made sure there'd be something or someone waiting for her when she got home. Like early in the morning. As their tickets out of Seattle had originally had them booked. But they'd caught a military flight out. Getting them home hours early. Cooper had made the arrangements. Had he canceled the original plans?

He checked the airlines. It still said Arianna was due to arrive at five-thirty am.

His instinct prodded him. What if someone planned for her to not make it home?

He wanted to take her out of here and back to his place now. He quickly dressed, that sense of something wrong riding him hard. He sent several more texts then turned his attention to sleeping beauty. Throwing back her covers, he went to the dresser and pulled out clothes for her.

"Arianna?" he said in a harsh whisper. "Get dressed. We're leaving."

Groggy after only a couple of hours sleep, she sat up and blinked at him.

He didn't waste any time with explanations but worked to get her clothes on her again. When she was up and ready to go, silent but awake, he carried her downstairs and out the back of the house.

She wrapped her arms around him and held on. He loved that she didn't bubble over with protest or questions. She trusted him at a level he'd never had anyone trust him before.

Outside he recognized the condos all shared the same back-yard. He kept close to the buildings and worked his way to the right, around the last one. The room was tight, but the sky was already getting lighter. He peered out onto the street. Then raced to his Jeep.

He set her down on her feet and unlocked his vehicle.

"Oh, I don't think so."

Shadow froze at the foreign sounding voice. He glanced at Arianna to see the horror on her face. And knew.

It was the missing so called terrorist who had turned to exhortation and kidnapping to fund his cause. Shadow turned slowly to see a handgun pointed directly at him. Shit.

"If you don't mind, we need you to get into that truck. We have a bit of a trip ahead of us."

Arianna shook her head. "No, I can't. No more."

"I could put a bullet in your friend here? Would that make you more cooperative?"

"No!" she cried. "I'll come." She glanced around blindly. "Where do you want me to go?"

"That truck." And he pointed to a black vehicle to the far side of the road. "Now."

Arianna stumbled forward, her leg stiff and ungainly. As she came close to the kidnapper, she fell.

He swore and reached out to stop her.

And Shadow was on him in an instant.

CHAPTER 23

A RIANNA LAY ON the pavement, her leg throbbing and watched as Shadow kicked the gun out of the man's hands and pounded his face into the ground. She didn't want him to kill the enemy, he had enough to deal with in his life. But she didn't want the asshole to get up again. She pulled herself along the ground to where the gun lay. She might not like them, but to save Shadow's life, she'd use it without a second thought. As she already had.

"Ha. Like you're going to get that."

And a foot stomped down on top of the gun in front of her.

She closed her eyes. Damn she'd been so close. She stared at her step–uncle. A man more a stranger than a relative. "Really? It was you all the time?"

He shrugged. "Well, not just me."

He nodded to the vehicle parked to the side. "Your step-mother might have had something to do with it."

If a heart could break, Arianna knew hers was at the point of trying. Her stepmother had her father killed? Together with her uncle? How…how…words failed her. With difficulty, she pulled herself up to stand then hobbled closer to face her stepmother. "You did that to him?" she said incredulously. "Why? You had everything."

"He was going to divorce me," Linda snapped.

Arianna shook her head. "So? That's hardly worth killing him for. He planned to divorce my mother, but she died before he could."

"And if she'd lived you'd have realized that he planned well for that contingency. She was going to be squeezed out completely. He wasn't going to give me anything either." She sneered. "You lucked out. Do you have any idea how shitty your life would have been if your mother had lived?"

"Money? This has always been about money? Not Father's job?"

The uncle shrugged. "Why not make it a dual purpose. There was a lobbying committee that did want your father to take a beating. But that wasn't enough for our purposes. He needed to die so we could have the inheritance."

She nodded numbly as if she understood. But honestly...there was no understanding this. "And Kevin? Did he not deserve a father?" She wanted to rail against a world that would now take Kevin's mother from him too. There's no way Linda could keep this secret. The SEAL's would hunt her down and take her out – one way or another.

Her stepmother's vicious voice snapped, "He was no father."

"Right, well he's the one Kevin had. Now he has to learn that his mother is a murderer."

"And who is going to tell him?" Linda said in harsh acerbic tones. "You won't be around to ruin him."

Ruin him. She'd have done anything to make that boy's life happy. Unlike his parents. "Is that why you needed me dead? So you didn't have to worry about Kevin loving me more than you?" she cried. "So you have to murder me?"

The stepmother laughed. "Absolutely not. I was never jealous of you, no need to be. Kevin doesn't love you," she said snidely. "But we need your money."

"My money?" Arianna stared at her in bewilderment. "I have some, but nothing like what you have now Father is dead."

It was her step–uncle who gave a bark of laughter at that comment. "That's where you're wrong. See, his estate goes equally to you and Kevin. And your estate when you die, goes to Kevin. So as his guardian, Linda and I will have complete control over all of it."

"And my brother?" She gazed from one to the other. "Will he ever see a penny of it?"

"Maybe. And maybe not. Depends on how long the money lasts."

She shook her head. She couldn't believe it. She'd been surrounded by the enemy. If she died, then there'd be no one there for Kevin. Did they know about her inheritance from her grandmother, on her father's side that left Kevin a sizable inheritance as well? If so they'd kill him too. She had little doubts that if it came to a competition between her son and money, Linda would choose the money.

She always had.

There had to be some way out of this mess. She glanced at the unconscious kidnapper on the street. "So is he a terrorist?"

"Well, yes and no. He bears a remarkable resemblance to a famous one so I knew the ruse would work." He sneered. "Sometimes you just have to act when you see the perfect opportunity." He lifted the hand gun. "The funny thing is, he's a little terrorist connected to a bigger one and they jumped all over this plan. Squeezed me about dry trying to get to this point. I'm happy there aren't any of them left. Less to pay at the end." He casually lined the gun up and pulled the trigger.

The unconscious man's body jerked.

Arianna cried out in a low voice, "He was unarmed."

"And now he's dead." Her step–uncle laughed. "Jesus, you're such a fool. None of you get to live this night out. Sorry about your boyfriend though. What did you do, pick him up at the airport?"

He laughed and lined the gun up on Shadow's head. "Now to make sure it looks like our terrorist shot your boyfriend first then killed himself."

He went to pull the trigger. Arianna screamed and dove in front of the gun but was slammed to the ground as gunfire lit the night.

Followed by a hushed silence.

Arianna lay on the ground, Shadow covered her as a blanket. Her stepmother was crying hysterically beside the vehicle. And her step–uncle…was lying in a pool of blood.

As sudden as the silence, there came the noise. Sirens, dogs barking, house lights came on.

And then the men.

Cooper. Mason. Dane. Hawk. Swede's big head above Shadow's.

"Arianna, you hurt?" Swede asked.

She shook her head, realizing she was bawling like an idiot. She sniffled and tried to stop the waterworks, but it wasn't until Shadow got up and hauled her gently up into his arms that she managed to slow it down. She wrapped her arms around his neck and squeezed tight.

"It's okay," he whispered. "You're safe."

She sniffled and looked at the men surrounding them. She let go of Shadow to walk into Swede's huge arms. Then each of the others as she hugged them hard.

Held safe and secure back in Shadow's arms, she said, "Thank you all so much."

"We were hardly going to desert you until it was over," Swede said. "Besides, Shadow here hasn't told us if he's keeping you."

"Keeping me?" she turned a puzzled look up to Shadow.

"Forget about it. It's a recurring joke among the men."

Shadow used such a dismissive tone, her suspicions were instantly aroused. She turned back to Swede for clarification, studied the huge grin on everyone's face, and thought about all she'd learned about the group. "As in a joke you all participated in and now it's Shadow's turn. Correct?"

Cooper laughed. "I said she was bright." And he nodded. "That's exactly right. Only Shadow and I are still unattached. So it's been a standing joke since Mason first met his partner. Now if anyone looks close to finding their perfect partner, we have to ask if he's keeping the woman in question. Because if not, there is always another one of us who might be interested." And he waggled his eyebrows in a mock leer.

She laughed. Then threw her arms around Shadow crying, "Keep me, please keep me."

"I never planned to do anything but that from the moment I met you," he whispered against her ear. "Some of us know exactly what we want and know to go after it."

With a happy cry, she hugged him tight. Then pulled back slightly and said, "I come with baggage, you know that, don't you?"

"Kevin?"

She nodded. "He's lost everyone else."

Shadow smiled. "No, he's gained six uncles."

She turned to look at the group of heroes smiling at the two of them. "He's going to love that," she said warmly. "He's had so very little male contact in his life."

"Oh," Mason said with a grin. "He'll get lots now."

Tears came to her eyes. It had been a hell of a trip. She'd lost her father, found out her stepmother had betrayed them all, and her step-uncle. Kevin would need years to get over this nightmare, and all she could think of as she stood there in Shadows arms – was that she was so damn lucky. She smiled up at him. "I'm so glad I went on that trip. It was the worst trip imaginable but as far as silver linings go... If I hadn't gone I'd have missed meeting you and that would have been horrible." She leaned up and whispered so only he could hear, "I love you so much."

"Not as much as I love you," he murmured and to the cheers of his team, he kissed her yet again.

This concludes Book 5 of SEALs of Honor: Shadow.

Book 6 is available.

Cooper: SEALs of Honor, Book 6

Buy this book at your favorite vendor.

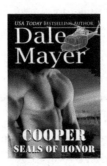

SEALs of Honor Series

Mason: SEALs of Honor, Book 1

Hawk: SEALs of Honor, Book 2

Dane: SEALs of Honor, Book 3

Swede: SEALs of Honor, Book 4

Shadow: SEALs of Honor, Book 5

Cooper: SEALs of Honor, Book 6

Markus: SEALs of Honor, Book 7

Evan: SEALs of Honor, Book 8

Chase: SEALs of Honor, Book 9

Brett: SEALs of Honor, Book 10

SEALs of Honor, Books 1–3

Author's Note

Thank you for reading Shadow: SEALs of Honor, Book 5! If you enjoyed the book, please take a moment and leave a short review.

Dear reader,

I love to hear from readers, and you can contact me at my website: www.dalemayer.com or at my Facebook author page. To be informed of new releases and special offers, sign up for my newsletter. And if you are interested in joining Dale Mayer's Fan Club, here is the Facebook sign up page.

Cheers,
Dale Mayer

COMPLIMENTARY DOWNLOAD

DOWNLOAD a *__complimentary__* copy of TUESDAY'S CHILD? Just tell me where to send it!

http://dalemayer.com/starterlibrarytc/

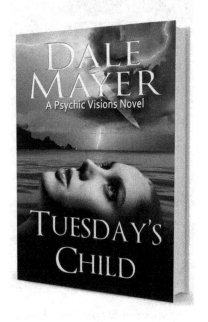

Touched by Death

Adult RS/thriller

Get this book at your favorite vendor.

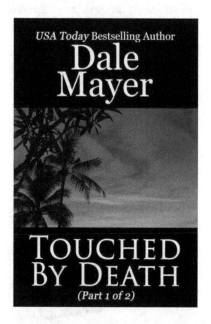

Death had touched anthropologist Jade Hansen in Haiti once before, costing her an unborn child and perhaps her very sanity.

A year later, determined to face her own issues, she returns to Haiti with a mortuary team to recover the bodies of an American family from a mass grave. Visiting his brother after the quake, independent contractor Dane Carter puts his life on hold to help the sleepy town of Jacmel rebuild. But he finds it hard to like his brother's pregnant wife or her family. He wants to go home, until he meets Jade – and realizes what's missing in his own life. When the mortuary team begins work, it's as if malevolence has been released from the earth. Instead of laying her ghosts to rest, Jade finds herself confronting death and terror again.

And the man who unexpectedly awakens her heart – is right in the middle of it all.

By Death Series

Touched by Death – Part 1
Touched by Death – Part 2
Touched by Death – Parts 1&2
Haunted by Death
Chilled by Death

Vampire in Denial

This is book 1 of the Family Blood Ties Saga

Get this book at your favorite vendor.

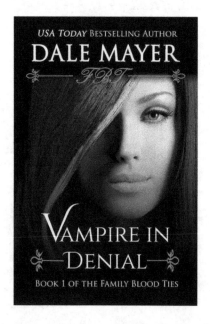

Blood doesn't just make her who she is...it also makes her what she is.

Like being a sixteen-year-old vampire isn't hard enough, Tessa's throwback human genes make her an outcast among her relatives. But try as she might, she can't get a handle on the vampire lifestyle and all the...blood.

Turning her back on the vamp world, she embraces the human teenage lifestyle—high school, peer pressure and finding a boyfriend. Jared manages to stir something in her blood. He's smart and fun and oh, so cute. But Tessa's dream of a having the perfect boyfriend turns into a nightmare when vampires attack the movie theatre and kidnap her date.

Once again, Tessa finds herself torn between the human world and the vampire one. Will blood own out? Can she make peace with who she is as well as what?

Warning: This book ends with a cliffhanger! Book 2 picks up where this book ends.

Family Blood Ties Series

Vampire in Denial

Vampire in Distress

Vampire in Design

Vampire in Deceit

Vampire in Defiance

Vampire in Conflict

Vampire in Chaos

Vampire in Crisis

Vampire in Control

Family Blood Ties 3in1

Family Blood Ties set 4–6

Sian's Solution – A Family Blood Ties Short Story

Broken Protocols

Get this book at your favorite vendor.

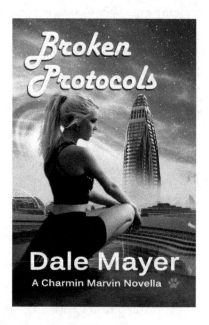

Dani's been through a year of hell...

Just as it's getting better, she's tossed forward through time with her orange Persian cat, Charmin Marvin, clutched in her arms. They're dropped into a few centuries into the future. There's nothing she can do to stop it, and it's impossible to go back.

And then it gets worse...

A year of government regulation is easing, and Levi Blackburn is feeling back in control. If he can keep his reckless brother in check, everything will be perfect. But while he's been protecting Milo from the government, Milo's been busy working on a present for him...

The present is Dani, only she comes with a snarky cat who suddenly starts talking...and doesn't know when to shut up.

In an age where breaking protocols have severe consequences, things go wrong, putting them all in danger...

Charmin Marvin Romantic Comedy Series

Broken Protocols

Broken Protocols 2

Broken Protocols 3

Broken Protocols 3.5

Broken Protocols 1-3

About the Author

Dale Mayer is a USA Today bestselling author best known for her Psychic Visions and Family Blood Ties series. Her contemporary romances are raw and full of passion and emotion (Second Chances, SKIN), her thrillers will keep you guessing (By Death series), and her romantic comedies will keep you giggling (It's a Dog's Life and Charmin Marvin Romantic Comedy series).

She honors the stories that come to her – and some of them are crazy and break all the rules and cross multiple genres!

To go with her fiction, she also writes nonfiction in many different fields with books available on resume writing, companion gardening and the US mortgage system. She has recently published her Career Essentials Series. All her books are available in print and ebook format.

Connect with Dale Mayer Online

Dale's Website – www.dalemayer.com
Twitter – @DaleMayer
Facebook – facebook.com/DaleMayer.author

Also by Dale Mayer

Published Adult Books:

Psychic Vision Series

Tuesday's Child

Hide'n Go Seek

Maddy's Floor

Garden of Sorrow

Knock, Knock…

Rare Find

Eyes to the Soul

Now You See Her

Psychic Visions 3in1

Psychic Visions Set 4–6

By Death Series

Touched by Death – Part 1

Touched by Death – Part 2

Touched by Death – Parts 1&2

Haunted by Death

Chilled by Death

Second Chances...at Love Series

Second Chances – Part 1

Second Chances – Part 2

Second Chances – complete book (Parts 1 & 2)

Charmin Marvin Romantic Comedy Series

Broken Protocols

Broken Protocols 2

Broken Protocols 3

Broken Protocols 3.5

Broken Protocols 1-3

Broken and... Mending

Skin

Scars

Scales (of Justice)

Glory

Genesis

Tori

Celeste

Biker Blues

Biker Blues: Morgan, Part 1

Biker Blues: Morgan, Part 2

Biker Blues: Morgan, Part 3

Biker Baby Blues: Morgan, Part 4

Biker Blues: Morgan, Full Set

Biker Blues: Salvation, Part 1

Biker Blues: Salvation, Part 2

Biker Blues: Salvation, Part 3

Biker Blues: Salvation, Full Set

SEALs of Honor

Mason: SEALs of Honor, Book 1

Hawk: SEALs of Honor, Book 2

Dane: SEALs of Honor, Book 3

Swede: SEALs of Honor, Book 4

Shadow: SEALs of Honor, Book 5

Cooper: SEALs of Honor, Book 6

Markus: SEALs of Honor, Book 7

Evan: SEALs of Honor, Book 8

Chase: SEALs of Honor, Book 9

Brett: SEALs of Honor, Book 10

SEALs of Honor, Books 1–3

Collections

Dare to Be You…

Dare to Love…

Dare to be Strong…

RomanceX3

Standalone Novellas

It's a Dog's Life

Riana's Revenge

Published Young Adult Books:

Family Blood Ties Series
Vampire in Denial

Vampire in Distress

Vampire in Design

Vampire in Deceit

Vampire in Defiance

Vampire in Conflict

Vampire in Chaos

Vampire in Crisis

Vampire in Control

Family Blood Ties 3in1

Family Blood Ties set 4–6

Sian's Solution – A Family Blood Ties Short Story

Design series
Dangerous Designs

Deadly Designs

Darkest Designs

Design Series Trilogy

Standalone
In Cassie's Corner

Gem Stone (a Gemma Stone Mystery)

Time Thieves

Published Non-Fiction Books:

Career Essentials

Career Essentials: The Résumé

Career Essentials: The Cover Letter

Career Essentials: The Interview

Career Essentials: 3 in 1